When *Love* Meets Ego

Praise for *I Will Love Once Again*

"...talks about love, heartbreaks and finding love again..."

—Hindustan Times

"...quoting real life fun-filled experiences at workplace, and fun times with friends..."

— The Tribune

"...an inspiration for those who are heartbroken..."

—Ajit Samachar

When *Love* Meets Ego

Krishna

Srishti
Publishers & Distributors

Srishti Publishers & Distributors
Registered Office: N-16, C.R. Park
New Delhi – 110 019
Corporate Office: 212A, Peacock Lane
Shahpur Jat, New Delhi – 110 049
editorial@srishtipublishers.com

First published by
Srishti Publishers & Distributors in 2016

10 9 8 7 6 5 4 3 2 1

Printed and bound in India

If you hurt me,
I will hurt someone...

The time is gone when love was light,
It was pure with intent bright.
The attractions, distractions and cheats were tale,
The feel to be with one was without fail.
To be in love was a miracle and light,
Losing someone was accepted with delight.
But things have changed so far,
When being fake and dishonest are at par.
The trust is gone, lust exists,
Thought to be in leisure persists.
Cheat on me and I will on someone,
The mind will play but the heart will run,
Swindling and deceiving will grow,
You will cry
When Love meets your Ego....

Acknowledgements

This book is dedicated to all my readers who eagerly waited for the sequel to *I Will Love Once Again*, for all their love and wishes; to the people I came across with broken hearts and lost hope.

I am thankful to my parents and sister for their love and support. Special thanks to Gowthaman Eswaramurthi who is the inspiration behind a cute character in this novel.

Thanks to all my loving friends: Simerdeep Singh, Puneet, Varun, Sharika, Shiven, Shraddha and Aseem for supporting me. A lovely thanks to Late Deepika Arora (Jojo), Pooja Singh, and Ramit sir during my tenure in Wipro and NIC days.

Srishti Publishers for being so encouraging and promoting my writing.

And all you readers, do send in your feedback at iwloa30@gmail.com.

OM SHANTI.

I Will Love Once Again

The journey started when recession was at its peak. The offer letter came late and before I joined an MNC in Pune, I got the news of my girl getting engaged and leaving me forever. But the idea was clear: to not curse the past or lament, but to find love once again.

So the search began again. I found Simer – a surdy guy who can make even the dead laugh with his one liners – and my handy roommates cum friends who assisted me in my journey of finding and falling in love again.

It would have been just a thought when I kept comparing every girl I met with Priety till I found Riya, who was an absolute contrast to the one I had loved. Soon we were dating and going through that golden phase of knowing each other, till I discovered that I was still searching for the past in the present. It was too late to realize what I was doing, and the day I thought of proposing to Riya went on to be her last day in my life. The journey never stopped. I got transferred to NCR and I boarded the train from Bandra to Delhi, leaving behind my past and lost love.

The Suicide Note

August 2010

It was still dark outside at 4.15 a.m. and it was raining heavily. I had the keys of her flat with me and I knew there was something wrong that might have happened as she had never seemed so weak to have committed such a horrendous act…

The sound of the falling raindrops was crystal clear. It seemed to be a never-ending shower with lightning striking before the thundering burst of clouds. It was a shocker for me; I could hardly imagine her not being with me anymore. I had only dropped her home yesterday.....

The door opened with a creak as I unlocked it. I switched on the lights and made my way straight towards her bedroom. My eyes were eagerly searching for something as I knew there must be a certain reason for her sudden act. I searched the drawer, under the table, her almirah, and her bags in the hope of discovering anything that could at least tell me what might have happened in the last twenty-four hours. I was about to leave empty-handed when I noticed a blue light blinking under the bed. I guessed it was her laptop.

I pulled it out from under the bed and kept it on my lap to check. Her mailbox was open and there were unsent mails in the outbox.

I was shocked to find that the first unsent mail had the subject: **'I am done – Goodbye forever'**. I double clicked to check the contents, but fearing someone might come, I copied the mail and saved it in my pen drive. It was then that the lights went off, and before I could read anything further, the laptop shut down too. Damn, it was only working with the charger on. I kept everything aside, ejected the pen drive and ran out in a flash.

Life in NCR

December 2009

It was a cold winter morning when I landed in the reverberant city of the north, the city full of forward-looking and forward-thinking individuals coalesced with traditional finesse. A city trying to pace itself with technological advances, and housing people from all over the nation, supporting them in earning their living.

The city famous for Chandni Chowk, which may not direct you to China, but has enough to get you everything you desire. The captivating Palika Bazaar, the scintillating Red Fort from which the PM addresses the nation and the charming India Gate where one feels pride in one's nation. The glorious historical monuments starting from Humayun's Tomb, to the high rising minaret Qutab Minar. The place which is not only famous for the key government houses along with the booming metro services that may ease your journey to a large extent, but also is the heart of India holding all the spices of life together – IT hub, Gurgaon, to the film city in Noida and extending its reach till Greater Noida and Ghaziabad provides a complete package. Yes, this is the city close to every heart. This is Delhi. The city famous for all kinds of girls – hot girls, not so hot girls, smart girls, average girls, sexy girls, Janakpuri girls, South Delhi girls... Dilli girls. And for the young and the bold, this place is not known by what you have done, what you are doing or what you will do; but by how many girlfriends or boyfriends you can handle, the affairs you have had, the girls you have nailed, the 'exes' you have dumped and the 'exes' that have dumped you and so on.

The train halted at the railway station and like the movie star King Khan, I also slung the bag on my back. Standing at the door, looking at the crowd that was shouting, running, screaming and, of course, not paying any attention to me. I was trying to feel the warmth of the city when I was pushed out of the train for taking a few extra seconds, making me realize that I was in a city where every second mattered and couldn't be wasted. My torrid expression after being pushed was not noticed by anyone. I was out and I could see my co-passenger lifting her bag as well. She waved me goodbye and after walking a few steps ahead of me, she turned back and gestured with a thumbs up, wishing me all the best. I realized I had to call my friend. Without hiring the coolie, I managed to drag my luggage out from the exit gate near platform number sixteen. I took an auto to Sector 22 in Noida where my friend was living.

I was not at all happy after being transferred from Pune to New Delhi. I had successfully completed my training in an MNC in Pune and after failing in three out of four exams, I was able to clear the overall percentage. I survived to get a project and was sent to the NCR location. Even though I am a north Indian guy, I had never preferred the north. But my manager there thought otherwise and no matter how much I wanted to reject the transfer and oppose my manager, my impressive percentage was not enough to make me fight my case. Beggars can't be choosers, so I gracefully accepted it. I was new to corporate culture, so there was no question of going against of my manager's email.

It was my first day in office at the new location in Greater Noida. I couldn't imagine how far they had chosen a place to construct the office. I was a bit nervous, and as usual, I was not only late but late, by four hours. It was to be the first meeting with the manager of the first project I had got in an MNC where discipline, integrity, values, morals and culture dominate. Oh gosh! I was truly scared and began thinking of all the possible reasons I would give when interrogated. I recalled all the weird reasons I used to come up with along with Simer in Pune. The trainers often used to believe or pretend to believe us at that time. So I decided to call Simer before I went on to report to my manager.

"*Oh kidda pai ki haal hai?* How are you Munnu Khan?" Simer shouted at once. Munnu and Chunnu Khan, these were our names for each other from none other than '*feautibully*' Punjabi dubbed Angrezi movies.

Whenever it comes to describing surdy guys, a *Punjabi sardar*, people do tend to take it for granted that one has to be funny, but trust me, not every surdy guy has an impeccable comic timing like my friend.

"I am fine, Chunnu Khan. How are you? I feel I am still in Pune and might see you coming out with a new chick, trying to woo her and ask her for a date."

"*Na veer, kithe.* I guess I am nothing much without you. With you I felt I could woo even Miss India! But jokes apart, oh wow!...a...a...featibul. See! Basically I am doing great and I will soon be a tech lead. Ya...ya...okay man...yup...will do that...yup yup.... My team will. I will simply fire that guy!"

He had suddenly raised his voice and started shooting off like a professional corporate lead. What nonsense!

"What's wrong with you? What are you saying? You are just a sixty-day-old chap and tech lead? Are you nuts?" I enquired.

"Oh *chup yar*... I mean shut up. A *totta* went and I don't know how I just deviated from the track, *waise* where I was?" Simer asked innocently. *Totta* in Punjabi means a ravishing chick.

"You were nowhere! You continue to impress and discourage yourself; it's my first day so I am leaving. Today I was just late by a few hours so will give some valid reason," I snickered and disconnected the call.

I was asked to report to the second floor. I was right there at the manager's desk. Before he could ask anything, I abruptly blurted out a reason.

"The bus I had taken dropped me far ahead and I had to struggle to find the office."

"I can understand. Whosoever comes here always struggles, so don't worry. But yes, better leave in the office cab. This area is not that safe. Follow me; I will introduce you to your team."

With my mouth half open to spout a few more excuses for my unpunctuality, I followed my new manager.

"I will give you an introduction to the project as well," he said keeping his phone in his left pocket. Swiping his card, he opened the cabin door.

"This is basically a government project and you will be a part of the global delivery organization team. We are into the 'national customs' domain. I guess you are trained in Pl/SQL and SQL and are competent to deal with this..." as he explained my role which obviously I was hardly listening to, my eyes scanned the bays and cabins, searching for a figure who would confirm my presence in the NCR.

"The team already has twelve members, and is really good to work with. They have joined last month. I guess they were one month ahead of your training batch, so meet your first teammate, Chiya…Chiya…Chiya!"

Busy explaining the project and describing the team, and pointing towards the right side of the bay, he didn't notice that only three people seemed to be alive. They were busy playing 2-D games on their respective assigned PCs. Few were missing and few were….

"Chiya….Chiya….Chiya...wake up!

The manager was left with no other option than to raise his voice to wake her up from her sound sleep. The remaining people minimized their windows, quickly began to hide the achievements of their respective games and tried concentrating and exploring their desktops.

"Why are you sleeping? Are you done with reading the document?" The manager popped another question. Rubbing her face, she struggled to open her eyes but managed to give a confident and innocent reply.

"*Hum kuch soch rahe the.* I was thinking something."

I looked at her in surprise and wondered about her innovative way of thinking and getting a solution with her PC still waiting to be turned on!

"I want you to give me a detailed review about the document by the second half and hope the team is ready with the presentation," the manager stated and gave a tormented look. Raising his eyebrows and looking at the team, he left for his cabin, leaving my introduction with the team in midstream. Self-intro is always a cranky task and I was about to leave when one of the active team members called me and introduced me to the whole team. That's when we were distracted by the loud snoring of someone in the next bay.

"Oh, he is Gowtham and he is always..."

One of the team members aimed a piece of roughly-folded paper at him.

"Dayam dayammm!! Illa illaa! Hey man, are you mad? Is this the way to behave with a citizen? You north Indiyans are mad...that is why saaaouth is good...maii Tamil is good..." he wailed and went out. I could hear him saying "Tamil is maii country. Idiots rascalaass" as he moved out of earshot.

I couldn't stop laughing, nor could the rest of the team. He was from Tamil Nadu and not at all happy in NCR. After completing his training, he was sent here while his remaining batchmates were shifted to Chennai. I guess all MNCs work by the divide and rule principle. He was a bespectacled guy with a wheatish complexion, average height and of course with a typical south Indian accent. He was scared of ghosts and spirits and was a firm believer that he was suffering from witch attacks. The rest of the members were from Orissa, a few from Mumbai and a majority of them from UP. Chiya whose excuse just reminded me of my training days in Pune was from Lucknow. I interacted with them for quite a while. The next boring step was to find a flat, PG or roommate. I was expecting the same kind of roommates as I had in Pune. On enquiring I came to know that most of the guys in the team were already well-settled. Gowtham was the only one staying alone as a PG. I was left with no option but to go look for the frustrated Gowtham. So I went out and located him near the pantry making a cup of tea.

I could see the frustration on his face, so was unsure whether he'd speak to me.

"Hi Gowtham! How are you?"I greeted him and introduced myself only to get a suspicious look from him. I looked at him and stated before he could leave.

"You know, I just hate it here. I never wanted to come to NCR. I love...I love the west aaa...south...yes south. I wish I could go to Bangalore or Chennai. You know, people are really good and soft hearted there," I said keeping an eye on his changing expression.

"And I guess the culture is totally different from here. People are polite and humble...and...a...." I continued before running short of words, and developing strain on my eyebrows for keeping an animated friendly expression.

"Hey man! Have you ever been to the saaouth? Maii Tamil Naaadu, Chhennnai? Tirupur maii loovlyyy district?" he interrupted and asked in excitement, swinging and swirling every word in his own direction.

"Aa...aaa unfortunately, I have never been to Tamil, but I have been to Kerala when I was two...but don't remember much about the place," I replied a little sheepishly.

"And I would love to visit Tamil, Chennai and Tripura," I added immediately.

"Oh man! It's not Tripura, it is Tirupur. And Kerala has no connection with Tirupur," he giggled asking me to correct my geography while checking someone else's geography. A splendid chick filling her cup of tea distracted him. I guess she cooled him down, else he might have thrown his cup of tea at me for calling Tirupur as Tripura.

We had a good conversation and I came to know more about him. He really seemed to be a simple guy but stubborn about his own principles. You can't expect him to behave according to your terms. At times he would give regard to my opinions but only on the matters related to him. Spending a few hours with him was fun as he was good company, funny in his own style. I also learned the three current important things in his life. First: he had a weakness towards the opposite sex. Second: he was also struggling to find a roommate and a place to stay as he was to vacate the place he was staying in at present. His choice was strictly a South Indian guy, unfortunately. The third was that he was scared of dogs, which may not be a current issue, but was his phobia. He was currently staying at Mayur Vihar Phase-3 and after promising to assist him to locate a new place, I convinced him to stay with me.

Flashback

Journey from Bandra to New Delhi

The beauty with cat-like eyes, her yellow-covered novel by Danielle, her stern look through her glasses. Her yellow top was a perfect fit, showing her curves without an inch of difference, as if she was the cover model of Femina. *My seat number was 32. The train was at Bandra station, Mumbai.*

I was travelling from Mumbai to Delhi. I met her when I was sitting on the wrong seat, and at a time when I had almost decided to end my search for love. That's what one does when he is unable to achieve any results about what he had decided a few months ago. The same old story of falling and failing in love, then falling and failing again. I guess we all have such experiences, so nothing new to elaborate. But just to enjoy what happened earlier, you can read I Will Love Once Again, *a national bestseller. Don't give me that severe look. Every author has the right to call his novel a bestseller. Now back to the train that I had boarded.*

She gave me a stern look through her glasses while introducing herself; her gaze pierced deep into my eyes. She wasn't rude though, as her body language might sound at first sight; maybe she had kept herself that way to keep strangers away. But she seemed sweet otherwise. The conflict began: whether to begin a conversation or not. I was a little bored trying to get her attention. I finally got it when she looked at me disgustingly when I knocked off her cell phone which she had kept on the edge of the seat. I could only smile apologetically in return, pretending ignorance, which I guess she found genuine enough to feel that I had not done it deliberately. She stopped frowning. This was the right time, so I began, and after a few formal introductory rounds, I fired the question or rather affirmed statement.

"I guess you are a Sagittarian or an Aquarian or Leo."

It might be an old and boring method of taking a conversation to the next level, talking about sun signs. Nevertheless, she smiled and adjusting her seat, took out her novel from her bag, which was vast, apart from the two huge VIP bags that she was carrying. I felt a little ignored but before I could ask again, she was gracious enough to reply.

"Try a few more times; I guess you will complete all the sun signs in the next two attempts," she said deflating my hopes of having guessed correctly. I could see the cover page of the novel she had taken out. The author's name was Danielle. She was at the window seat and I could notice the jogging tea vendors getting off the running train as the train left the platform.

An hour passed by and something was irritating me. Why wouldn't one be irritated when you know the girl sitting next to you is someone who has a natural tendency of being relaxed while making boys suffer from the habit called ogling! I was not sure whether to consider myself fortunate getting a seat next to her, or curse the fact that I couldn't look at her as she might feel offended. Finally, after a few hours, when I found her relaxing her eye muscles, I took my chance.

"I guess this is the same book where the girl falls in love with the wrong guy who cheats on her, making her life hell, and finally

she commits suicide," I said in one go, behaving as if I had decoded something which she was still figuring out.

I thought I had done a great job by highlighting my knowledge about the book she was reading, then for a second I thought I had snubbed her by revealing the death of the girl which she might be getting attached to. All this tickled within a few seconds in my mind. She took the bookmark somewhere from the initial pages and with firm calmness, slid it between the pages she had been reading.

"You spoiled the suspense, don't you think you should learn to sit quiet," she replied with utter calmness as if she was talking to a five-year-old kid.

"No...I was...trying to...oh helping you..." I stammered trying to choose my words carefully with fluttering lips, visibly nervous.

"And did I ask for any help?" she asked staring through her glasses with a straight face.

"Not at all, no... You didn't," I replied sheepishly.

"Good! Now you..." before she could put an end to our conversation, I cut her short.

"Obviously...who would waste time reading something when you know it's just a plain suicidal story. Such cases are totally irrational when you find a girl falling for the wrong guy. They should not choose the one who is double crossing them," I don't know what I said and how quick it was, but she sat up.

"I like guys who are like that. Do you mind? And I have the least concern about the girl in the story. I like the guy's character which is feisty, strong and macho," she stated moving forward from her chair. She removed her glasses which I found were just anti-glare. She stared at me and I was in an 'I might piss-in-my pants' kind of situation. I recollected my statement as I had not given a thought about what I had said a minute ago.

'What kind of a girl are you?' I wanted to ask her as I thought she was too practical, not at all emotional and hard-hearted. One who liked guys who were Casanovas, or studs. 'Are you serious? I mean are you the kind of a girl who would love to be cheated on or one who'd enjoy multiple affairs?' I thought.

"Now you must be thinking something cheap about me," she stated getting a little fierce, just like the kind of character she liked in the book. But how did she know that I was thinking along that line. Was I too predictable? Perhaps my weird expressions and blank stare had convinced her of that.

"Yess...no...noo...I mean no...I was just..."

"What were you thinking then?" she interrupted me in between and asked again as if she wanted to know more. For a moment I thought why did I speak to her? It would have been fine if I had limited myself to just gawking at her, or even better, ignoring her. It was like I just had a red chili. Gosh! Her cheeks were red, she was looking cute – in fact red hot. But that was just her looks, not her inclination towards me.

Gaining some confidence with little fear of getting thrashed if she shouted or just raised her voice, I said, "I mean to say that everyone wants a perfect love story, every girl seeks someone true and honest. Why you are against all this? It's like you are the leader of anti-one-woman-men or a mahila mandal who is just against the guys who are fine with one."

She gave me a piercing look but then burst into laughter. For a moment she seemed like someone else.

"You are funny...mahila mandal! Oh god!" she said laughing. When I realized I was with the same girl, I closed my open mouth and changed my nervous expression. I gave a smile and gazed confidently as I patted my back. I had transformed her into a laughing Buddha.

Her flawless skin shimmering, her white teeth sparkling, her eyes glowing and now her jovial mode bowling me over.

"By the way...I am Shikha," she introduced herself again and we had another introductory round. This was better than the formal one. It was lunch time and we had our lunch together. We ate some stuff well packed in a hot case given to her by her maternal aunt. I came to know more about her. She was from Lucknow, the city of nawabs. She had finished her B.Com recently and was preparing for an MBA. From New Delhi, she would be travelling further to her hometown in an hour's time. She enquired a little about me as well. I remembered that she had said she preferred feisty, macho or Casanova kind of men. Clearly, I was still stuck with the same thought which she had highlighted a while ago. I asked her about the same when she changed her expression and replied in a stiff tone.

"Yes, I like guys like those. In fact, I am a girl who doesn't believe in a single affair. If you guys can, then even we have the right to play with you."

I stared at her in a state of incomplete admittance to what she was avowing. I hadn't been in touch with any girl so blunt and aggressive. Though my expression was held firm with a straight face, trying hard to not react, but inside me, my veins, arteries, and each and every delicate part started performing like the serviced motor engine without any engine oil.

I perhaps started thinking about her being with me; of course it was not love as I was quite mature. It wasn't like what I had been doing in Pune – seeking love in every girl before boarding the train. However if a sweet, beautiful, hot girl sitting next to you, talking to you or sharing lunch and even smiling at you, automatically gives you a signal that she is interested in you...it's called 'I-got-her' kind of poor guys logic. I seemed to be suffering from the same misconception.

"Why should you guys have all the fun? I am having fifteen affairs and I guess I am cheating on many. I hope that's okay," she stated untying her hair and letting it fall lose on her thin, firm shoulders. I was concentrating hard to not look anywhere else and just to maintain an eye contact with her, or perhaps looking out of the window. But The 'fifteen boyfriends' line gave me a hiccup and that was pretty clear to her. I felt like I had failed in some kind of an exam. I didn't know how to react, so a question mark automatically surfaced on my straight face.

She stared at me and could notice my dead face before she burst into laughter again. This time people sitting around couldn't resist staring at us. Some out of curiosity lifted themselves from their seats to check what was so funny.

"Arre buddhu… I am just kidding. Which Indian girl has a liberty to cross all barriers?" I must say I felt a little relieved as if she had disclosed a suspense that would have decided my future. And she continued, "And even if I did, why should I share that in public or in front of a stranger?"

Now this was like a boomerang that hit me hard and went straight back to her manicured hands with the silver pearl ring. What did she mean by saying that I was a stranger to her? I knew her rather well, how could I be a stranger then?

"I mean I hardly know you," she said as though reading my thoughts.

Now that sounded a little interesting. She wanted to know me, and my hopes rose. How we guys immediately come to a conclusion and stay positive within ourselves that 'She' might be interested if a girl is conversing with us.

"The truth is that I like someone. Now please don't give me that look. He was from my college so he recently proposed to me," she stated with a glow in her eyes, adding to the dismal look in my eyes.

"So what did you say?" I asked in a single breath.

"Aaah... so fast, why should I tell you?" she asked and seemed a little unwilling or pretended to be so.

Then why was there a need to tell me that, I thought but couldn't say it to her. Instead, I stated with an indifferent look, "Nothing, it's just you are sharing your thoughts and I am listening to kill time. It's fine if you don't want to," I said and without looking at her, I pretended to check messages in my phone as if to maintain the 'I have a life' kind of look. It was as though the rising mercury level saw a dip with her sudden admittance about her love or whatever.

"The fact is...I am confused about him," she stated twirling a strand of her hair. Now I was back again, as if the same mercury level suddenly rose to a mark that 'you are still alive'. I pretended to have completed my task of replying to the messages and put my phone back in my pocket, steadily curbing my excitement to know what was in her mind about the idiot who had proposed to her.

"He is a nice guy, smart, intelligent...but I guess something is missing." The last bit of her sentence made me smile. Inside my mind, I seemed to be flying as though she'd be saying 'I like you' to me the next moment, a typical guy.

"You are thinking too much. You should relax and if he is a nice guy, you should give him a chance. You never know what and where your story can go!"

Like a perfect analyst, I offered my suggestion, confident about the fact that whatever I suggest, girls will do the opposite. I was acknowledging myself and was expecting a reply in my favour.

She thought for a second, and looked at me and smiled. I smiled as well.

"I guess you are right. I should say yes to him, I think I like him too." she stated in excitement as I turned my smile to a frown and sneaked my hand in my pocket to check my cell again. Nonsense!

It was close to 11.00 p.m. and I could see her feeling heavy-eyed as she finished the last page of a chapter from the novel. She was reading it despite the fact that I had ruined the suspense. Then she gathered her things, lifted her legs off the floor and folded them. She draped herself in a warm shawl. Before wishing me goodnight, she advised, "I must say you should never fall into anything in a hurry, better to just kill time, or engage in time pass affair." She winked and smiled.

I pretended as if I had been interrupted from a very important thought and asked her to elaborate on the word 'anything'.

"Anything like 'falling in love', 'searching for love' and so on." She stated in a quiescent tone which I found very striking. I wanted her to keep talking. Her stress on 'falling in love', 'searching for love' hit me.

How did she have an inkling of what I was thinking or was it just a generic statement hitting the right button? I kept on listening after nodding at her.

'See, you are going to Delhi, so have fun, find chicks, make girlfriends but don't get serious because if you lose, then your ego will defeat your love when you find your love encountering your ego. You will only be left struggling and stranded with nothing but regret."

I was just staring at her and had nothing to say when she whispered moving an inch closer, putting a little more stress on her words to make it sound clear.

"*It hurts* when love meets ego."

I looked at her in disdain and was waiting for her to burst into laughter and say 'kidding re'. We however just made eye contact and she turned her head in the other direction and dozed off after a wink.

There was silence as she slept for a while after gazing out of the window. She might have been thinking about that boy, or might have been considering him as an option or maybe not thinking of either. I was reassessing her words 'when love meets ego'. I felt even she must have been hurt, or her ego dominated her love, but I was least concerned about that.

The full moon outside spread its blue light outside the window. The dark trees running in the opposite direction highlighting the speed of the train, the dim light inside and the beauty sleeping next to me, the turning of her head towards my side, and her hair falling over her cheeks. For a moment everything went still and a cool breeze suddenly started to flow into the bogie. The moon light falling on half her face dazzled her radiant skin, the distance between us was just reduced to a millimeter with her head resting on my shoulders. She opened her eyes for a moment and we were lost in each other. A scene so perfectly scripted like a movie, truly unrealistic.

It happened only in my dreams. Instead, it was pitch dark outside with no moon, people snoring nearby, poor light in the bogie and she was in deep sleep with her head resting against the window seat, leaving me pondering on the thought of 'when love meets ego'.

I was just evaluating her emphasis on having a girlfriend for fun but not for love. How was that possible? Two people who are close can be in love of course, but can I be in a relationship without love? I will try that. Now I had to find someone without love. Would I be able to? Would I have to tell someone that you are with me just to kill time? Or will my real intentions be depicted in my eyes? If everybody was having fun, then I could as well, I thought as I closed my eyes.

It was a cold winter morning when I landed in the reverberant city of the north. I was out on the platform after being pushed off the train. I could see Shikha lifting her bag as she waved me goodbye. Walking few steps ahead of me, she turned back and gestured with her thumbs up, wishing me good luck. I smiled and reminded myself of the task assigned unintentionally to me. I lifted my bag, took out my Ray-Ban shades, and with the smile of a typical Bollywood movie actor on my face, I marched ahead to begin my search…

The Search Begins

Mayur Vihar Phase-3, Delhi

The search had never been so difficult in Pune, and I had found good friends and roommates. It was a tiring search for both of us, but we finally managed to find a nice room. It was on the third floor, above a clinic which was apparently an abortion centre owned by a widow. She had a beagle that was cute as we were told by her lady attendant. The room was to be converted into a girls PG accommodation soon as the clinic was on the verge of closing. They however found that no girl was willing to accommodate on the third floor, and we both quickly jumped in. We managed to convince the two attendants, but the daunting task was to talk to the lady doctor who was blunt, harsh and sometimes hyper as was conveyed to us.

"So you are the two guys?" she said placing herself on the chair behind the desk.

"Yes, ma'am," I said giving her a blank look.

Gowtham jumped in, "*Seri seri*… okay okay."

The old lady said, "But we want only girls. We can't accommodate you and…"

Gowtham burst out in part exasperation, part excitement, "What is this? This is not fair. You can't do this. I have to shift, previous owner is a rascala. If you come to saooth, maii saooth, we are great hosts. Tamil is always receptive…and Tirupur is maii…"

Her dog suddenly came into the room and stood next to Gowtham. He began losing his focus and stopped speaking mid-sentence. I saw the fear in his eyes as he shifted towards my right, slowly stirring from behind. The doctor seemed perplexed at Gowtham's behavior but she couldn't understand what the real reason behind his confusion was.

I took control over the situation and said, "He means that we are comfortable shifting to the third floor and I guess girls may be reluctant. We are new to this city and we will definitely pay you the rent on time. We got your reference from Dr. Srikant, by the way."

Gowtham sharply turned his neck towards me and nodded.

Looking at our desperate faces, she thought for a moment, looked at her attendants and then she said, "I have already refused a few boys but you both seem fine to me and since you have been sent by Dr Srikant, I can't say no."

She paused unzipping her purse only to take out a few biscuits for her beagle who was constantly staring at us without wagging his tail.

"Both of you can shift anytime, but keep this thing in mind that a few girls will be shifting to the second floor and they are coming next week and…"

Next week…. next week...next week.

That was enough to give us a ray of hope. We were definitely at the right place. It was as if some kind of energy booster in her last statement had widened our eyes and jammed our ears. Hearing her words we smiled at each other, a glitter in our eyes which only we could notice. We were startled from our explicitly generated series of wild thoughts when we finally heard her last sentence which I guess she had repeated twice.

"...is it clear...is it clearrrrrrr?"

Her dog's eyes were glued on us and any contradictory answer from us would result in us being bitten.

"Yes...yes clear. Don't worry," Gowtham nodded and agreed.

She stood up and started to move upstairs and her dog finally wagging his tail, followed her quietly. It gave us a parting look that seemed to say *'Now that you are staying here, I will see you later guys!'*

"I hate daags," Gowtham whispered.

"Excuse me, ma'am!" I called her. She paused and raised her eyebrows.

"By the way, what's his name?" I said pointing towards the dog.

"Oh! He is Scooby."

She smiled and disappeared. We came out and energized ourselves with some fruit juice near the street corner.

"You scared me man! And tell me who is Dr. Srikant and when did he refer us?" Gowtham asked.

I smiled and pointed to my right. His eyes followed my finger to the white board on a pole that read:

'Dr. Srikant's Clinic: Obstetrician and Gynaecologist'

"Oh thank god she didn't ask for any details. Poor lady...I think she is new in this PG business," he giggled.

"*Aahhh...naai naai....*"

Suddenly he shouted, scaring the customers standing nearby.

"What *naai naai*? And why are you petrified of barbers? Bloody, they are called naai naai...." I lashed, quickly sipping the juice and keeping the glass on the stand.

"Oh no dude! See that street dog behind you...I am frightened of dogs...hell how will I deal with that lady's scoundrel Scooby?

'Naai' meant 'dog', now I got it.

"Oh don't worry about that dog, we will befriend him," I stated with a straight face only to get inquisitive look from Gowtham.

"Dogs love to eat, and we will feed him something every day till he becomes our friend. I will show you."

He didn't seem convinced as I sped to the nearby general store and got a packet of glucose biscuits. I started calling the street dog that had terrified Gowtham.

"What are you doing man? I will kill you..." he said hiding behind me.

"Oh wait, you should always talk to dogs and feed them. Wooing them is like stealing candy from a baby. Look, he will take the offerings from us," I said as I presented him with a biscuit, only to get a stare in return. Seeing this, Gowtham started laughing and that actually made me conscious. I had to ignore Gowtham to concentrate on the dog.

"Aahhh...stealing candy...this *naai* is ignoring you."

"Tommy...Tommy...eat it. Scooby...Scooby...we will feed you every day," I said but in vain as he didn't move an inch. For a moment I was scared that he might jump on me and bite me, so I became a little attentive. With stifling expressions I took a bite of a piece myself and threw the other half at him. Before Gowtham could say anything, the dog quickly gobbled it up. He was wagging his tail as if inviting me to feed him again. I threw a piece again but he didn't touch it. When I bit another one and threw the remaining half, he grabbed it.

"That's cool man! He is only eating your half, I can see two dogs eating the same biscuit," Gowtham jumped in excitement and giggled making fun of my achievement.

I don't know how but I did manage to convince him that we can befriend any dog; he also made an effort and fed the dog. His fear seemed to have evaporated as he fed another dog and tried chatting with them. I am sure he must be convincing them stating *maai tirupur, maai tamil, maai district maai biscuits..maai daags....*

The team was almost ready and was waiting for me to join so that they could start the training. The manager was ready with the manual to be dictated to us. The guys seemed to be over enthusiastic as all of them were newcomers. I felt like the odd one out who was still feeling the injustice of not being in Pune with Simer and the others. My current team was excited to be shifted to the client's side as conveyed by my new manager Mr Tej Ghosh. He was six feet tall with a fair complexion and thinning hair – proof of his experience and age. He was good in dictating things and his stern appearance made sure that one could not think of even sneezing. The black mole under his right eye reminded me of Teja in the movie *Andaaz Apna Apna* and the scene in which Paresh Rawal says '*Mark idhar hai, Teja main hu*'. The team was just nodding to what he was saying and he emphasised on moving to Laxmi Nagar, NIC customs office where we would be handling the project. As I listened to him, I reminded myself of my task of finding a girl. I started scanning my team once again; there were few girls, but honestly, most of them were failing the criteria, and before I could scan any further…

"Excuse me, Mister…" my manager asked, bringing me back to the session I was attending.

"Aren't you a part of the team and interested in shifting to the client location?" I said nothing but nodded like all the other ten heads around me. The manager ended with an enthusiastic speech, and the team winded up the session to break for lunch.

"Excuse me, you left your notebook," Chiya stopped me and before answering her I thought about my last meeting with her. She was the same girl who was sleeping while the manager was introducing me.

"*Tum thode gayab ho kya?* Are you feeling lost?" she asked me.

"No, not at all," I replied confidently, fearing her a little. She seemed to be our team leader. She said nothing and left the cabin with a smile that clearly indicated that she had found me stupid. While leaving she bumped into Gowtham who was walking lost in his thoughts.

"*Kahan dhyan hai? Dekhte nahi hum jarahe hain?* Pay attention to where you're going," she sneered at him and before he could say anything, she stormed off in a hurry.

"Stupid girl! It was clearly her fault. Bloody naarth Indians."

Gowtham saw me and pretended as if nothing had happened; but he noticed my silly grin and he couldn't resist yelling about her for the next ten minutes. I came to know from him that Chiya was from Lucknow, from a well-settled and deep-rooted cultured family of nawabs owning acres of land. Her father carried the legacy of the Singhs and held the major reins on the town they were settled in. She had inherited the habit of calling herself 'hum', an honored version of 'I'. In short, she was a confident girl who held that supremacy in her language and attitude. Yet she was grounded. Dusky complexion, healthy build with sharp eyes, she was lively and had a shrill voice; you could hear her even if you were sitting a kilometer away. She was in a long term relationship with a guy and the guy was as good as one could expect a guy to be. They were planning to get married within the next three months.

We shifted soon after the doctor gave us the green signal. It was just a single room with an attached bathroom, good enough for guys who are new to the corporate earning culture. The lady attendant named Raajshri was in service since the day she got married. Her two kids had almost completed their metric exams now. She showed us the room which she honestly confessed to have opened after three years and a chunk of garbage including decayed wooden furniture was moved out and cleaned. The sharp odor of the cockroach and mosquito repellant was enough to convince us that they have worked hard to convert the old maternity ward room into a guest room. It was a tough ask to stand in the room for even a second. The walls were patchy and the cupboard doors had been left open to ventilate the insides. The ceiling fan was well polished but the switch near the door was half broken. Gowtham took his handkerchief out and started sneezing; the lady looked at him sideways and said, "You can shift elsewhere if you have a problem with the room." She spoke as if she had been given full authority to cancel the deal finalized by the owner herself.

Before Gowtham could say anything offending to the lady in charge, I intervened.

"It's perfect; where else could we find such a refreshing place and that too at decent rate."

I pinched Gowtham and pacified him.

"The only *guuud* thing about Delhi is that we will for eternity never be short of beauties around us," Gowtham stated staring at the girl in shorts, who moved in to the metro station with us, definitely ignoring us as if she knew that she had given us a topic to discuss at the Mayur Vihar metro station. We got our smart cards issued, and before we could take the escalator, Gowtham frowned.

"Aah.. *kodomay* mismatch!"

"What mismatch?" I asked puzzled.

"*Kodomay…ko-do-may* means *haarible.* Why do I have to state clearly what you can notice clearly?" He shouted at me.

"Oh horrible," I thought and decided not to correct his pronunciation.

"…And the worst part about Delhi is that all the beauties will be with a security guard and that guard will be her *baayfriend,*" he wailed as I saw the same girl in white shorts hugging her guard, I mean her boyfriend. He felt further mortified and I could see where the word *kodomay* appplied. The girl was cute, while the less said of her boyfriend the better.

"I love my Tirupur; good culture and no hugging and showing of emotions at my place. Girls look better in dresses…" he could see them following us on the next elevator towards the platforms.

"Ya man, relax. Why are you getting pissed off? It's simply called the law of role reversal."

"What's that? Could you please elaaborate?" Gowtham asked.

Meanwhile we had boarded the train and the couple who had offended Gowtham also got in with us. I could see the guy holding her left hand, resting on the opposite door, and girl standing holding the support. We both positioned ourselves in the middle just at the centre of two opposite doors. I could see Gowtham still trying to gape at the girl, but as he turned towards the skinny figure holding her hand, he would grimace.

"The law of role reversal is nothing but a feeling of pleasure by placing yourself in someone else's boots the moment you feel offended," I said staring out through the running metro which had just started.

"If you would have been with that girl, then any other guy watching you would have felt the same way. You'd be just a guard or a gardener for them." I giggled.

It was Saturday evening and as I looked around, the couples around me seemed restless. They were all on their way to hang out, date and have fun. Those in relationships seemed lost in the warmth of the metro while amateur couples seemed self conscious and coy. Young people in groups were busy discussing all the events at tuition centers, colleges, and schools. The middle-aged crowd was silent. Some had ear phones plugged in their ears thinking and imagining a better version of life with the rhythm of the song they were playing, while a few were staring at the youth blankly, smiling and trying to imagine what they were like at this age. Those who were left were like us, either finding faults in the couples or searching for wandering souls like ourselves, but definitely in the opposite sex.

"I didn't understand anything about that law of reversal, but I am sure this girl is not happy with this guy," Gowtham said swinging in between the passage.

"How can you say that I asked dividing my looks between Gowtham and the couple.

"I think the girl wants to be with me. I noticed her expression clearly stating that she committed a mistake by saying yes to this guy," Gowtham affirmed persistently staring at the girl, forgetting that she was with someone. I could see her holding hands and trying to get cozy with her boy playing with her phone. I guess her glance at Gowtham had made him confident about her. That proved that how positive he could be even after receiving a defiant look from the girl.

I have been to Delhi many times. My uncle used to stay in Delhi way back when I was a school going boy. I was never fascinated by Delhi; you will often find people saying that Delhi is fast, things move fast, people are smart, little brash, unproductive and flashy. I was wondering how fast life can be when I noticed the guy changing his expression to a sardonic look and holding the girl's hand tightly. For a second I thought he would hug her or do something cheesy, but the firmness in the hold suggested possessiveness with the hint of a little aggression. He said something that made that cute girl try to snatch her phone from him. The boy remained unmoved. Gowtham and I shared a look. What was going on? A part of the crowd shifted their eyes on them.

'Next station is Noida sector -18. Doors will open on the right.'

The announcement was bang on time and people prepared to disembark. We were also being pushed with the flow but I was little curious to know what would happen next. We however lost the sight of the couple. We flashed our smart cards at the exit and moved out from the gate closer to the GIP mall. Before we could take the stairs, I could see the couple near the exit stairs. They seemed to be settling things that had gone out of control a while ago.

"How can you cheat on me? He has written that he is missing you? Can you explain that?" he said as he wiped the sweat off his face in despair. Before we could hear the girl's explanation, I pushed Gowtham and we moved on.

"Where are you lost, Gowtham? We are getting late."

We moved ahead and turning my head back could only notice the girl trying to pacify him with a little disgusted look. Maybe she was feeling conscious about a scene being created. The sound of conversation washed out and running crowd discolored my view of checking on what happened next. I know that it was stupid of us peeping into other people's lives, but that was something Gowtham had never witnessed before. I have seen couples fighting, and many times I had been questioned when I was in a relationship, but for Gowtham it was something new. And never in front of a crowd at the metro station. I was thinking about how the journey between the few stations changed the relationship. Had they been fighting fifteen minutes back, Gowtham would have confirmed that the girl was fighting with the guy because she had fallen in love with him.

It was time to pay attention to my 'leisure hunt'. If I leave Gowtham, even I was stuck on an underprivileged thought of discovering someone I could date, as per the notion of 'Leisure hunt' given by Shikha. But honestly, what kind of bizarre search was it. We all are moving in life with such a thought. Who wants to be single when you know you have ample time to find and date someone. So it was on, but finding someone by walking on the streets, or roaming in a mall, or booking tickets or hanging in the metro to keep an eye on girls who were travelling with their so called baadyguards was all nonsense. But with Gowtham, the search was fun. Gowtham was being positive about everyone around him, imagining a perfect match for me and himself.

"*Intha ponnugale ippadi thanda,*" Gowtham said confidently. He looked at me and translated.

"All girls are the same…bus, train *madhiri onu poonaa innonnu varum*, so no worries."

He went on rambling, but I couldn't get anything. I was left with a big question mark with not so soothing expressions when he translated.

"I mean to say that they are like a bus, or a train. One will go, another will come, so no worries man!" he exclaimed.

"Oh, even you south Indians have the same thought. Wow!" I said amused and giggled.

"Ya man! It's universal law, but it's naat saaouth Indians. That's my Tamil, my Tirupurr, my lovely district. Do you mind?"

He expressed loudly, catching the attention of the people close by.

And It Happened...

"*I will kill you, Agent Smith...Agent Smith, you can't kill Rajni.*" "*I will kill you, Agent Smith...Agent Smith, you can't kill Rajni.*"

"Who is this fucking Agent Smith?"

I woke up half asleep trying to gain consciousness. Rubbing my eyes, I tried to locate my cell phone. It was three o'clock. I turned my head towards Gowtham to find him staring at me. Gosh! He scared me.

"Are you awake?" I asked him getting a little nervous, but he got up at once and asked.

"Where is Smith?"

He was being really weird. He didn't seem to recognize me and called me Morpheous, and he called himself Agent Neo. I suddenly recalled what my teammates had told me about his witch attacks. But I guess he had a sleeping disorder called Somniloquy; in simpler words, he was sleep-talking. I guess he was in Matrix mode, but where did Rajni figure in that. He might have mixed tamil movie and matrix together. I pointed in the other direction and he followed my finger, only to turn towards his bed, close his eyes and doze off.

There was a knock on the door. I opened my eyes when I found the knock a little harder and irritating. It was 9.00 a.m.

on Sunday. I searched for my slippers and opened the door to find Raajshri, the same woman who had shown us the room, standing there.

"Someone wanted to see you," she said giving me an impish smile. Rubbing my half-open eyes, I heard another voice.

"Hi, I am Eva. Aunty told me that two guys were staying on the third floor, so I thought I must meet them. We should know who our neighbors are, right?"

My blurred vision cleared and zoomed in on the figure standing next to Raajshri aunty. I shook my head to check what I was seeing was for real. It was clear. I could see a figure wearing peach coloured shorts with long waxed legs, a deep necked light grey top ending just above a pierced belly button and a body as clean and smooth as one after a shower and body lotion. The chilly morning with no sun had no effect on the girl who was covering herself with a cardigan long enough, finishing above her knees. Her wet hair and shining drops of fresh bath water were merging perfectly with the foggy weather outside. She was holding an armful of clothes which I guess were put to dry in the verandah last night. She was standing and leaning on her left leg. I could see all sorts of variety that were latest in fashion or trendy wrinkled, strangled and left half dead in her right hand. But I was awake now, as conscious as if put on an ATM duty. I confidently introduced myself and told her about Gowtham who was snoring loudly. He sounded like a howling wolf. Eva and aunty couldn't resist giggling.

"Ya, it was good you took the initiative. At least we can all turn to each other if anything is ever needed," I replied as genuinely as one could be.

She told me about her roommate Medha who worked even on Saturdays, and if required, on Sundays as well. Eva was from Agra. She had completed her MBA in HR from a not so recognized institute. Her face frowned on asking about the university. But if you observe, that's what we are all doing: studying what the herd is, getting admissions in numerous self-acclaimed number one institutes and then hardly respecting the university and being ashamed of naming it, admitted Eva with a straight sad face. My eyes tried not to look down below her chin or her glossy body. While chatting, she dropped one of the clothes she was holding. Before I could react to it and assist her, she bent down quickly, revealing more than what one could desire. Her deep neck top was loose enough to show a cream-coloured strapped new fashioned bra. The perfect shapes that I witnessed unwillingly resulted in my eyes going wide opened and made me feel like releasing heat through my ears.

Shifting my eyes somewhere else and pretending to have witnessed nothing, I just smiled when she said, "These bras are as slick as my relation with my guy," she stated something out of context but it was her capricious thought in a flow. Maybe she was conscious that I saw her private fabric or maybe she was just too talkative and blunt to hide even a pinch of emotion. I was startled by her offhand candour. I pretended to take no notice and instead turned around to check if Gowtham was up. I just smiled as I turned to her again.

"It was cool meeting you, buddy. See ya soon," she chirped and shook my hand before leaving. I stayed reliving the moment. How electrifying it was! I had already started thinking about her. How quick I was. She was nothing like Priety or Riya... the former my lost love and the latter whom I lost before realizing it was love. I was done looking for my lost love in every girl. Eva might turn out to be my hot girlfriend. Wow!

Laxmi Nagar - V3s Mall

The team of ten shifted to Scope Minar near V3s Mall, Laxmi Nagar. We were all relieved as we found this new location closer and more suitable, as it was in the city itself. We could see a healthy crowd around unlike the out-of-the-way, deserted Greater Noida. The only drawback of the new place was the office which was like a typical civil hospital building: the elevators were as old as the Delhi fort walls, painted and designed with regular pan splatter by government officials who were feeling pleased after handing over their chunk of work to us. They were our respective clients, and whatever they did and demanded, we had to oblige. Those were the instructions engraved in our MNC's nomenclature.

"Oh no! *Kodomay* washrooms," Gowtham expressed his grief while entering the loo. He was right. Atrocious it was and stinking like hell. The sinks were jammed and poor drainage systems made sure that the floor of the washroom was always wet. This was the state of all government office restrooms perhaps.

"Enaku kastakalam da unkuda," Gowtham said something in Tamil.

"What do you mean?" I asked with a weird face.

"I am having worst time since the time I have met you." Gowtham hollered at me. I gave him a startled look and he explained.

"I got a stinking room with you at that poor maternity ward, then this government hospital of an office and now these filthy washrooms," he pointed looking at me through his grey frames, his eyes wider than normal and eyebrows raised, while we were fixed against the wall releasing ourselves in the washroom. I paid little attention to his remarks, knowing his nature of shouting and blabbering at anything without any reason. I kept a straight face.

It's easy to change his line of thought so I asked him, "Which films did you watch during this weekend?" I zipped my jeans to move towards the pan splattered washbasin.

"What does that have to do with the tough time I am having with you?" he asked finishing his quota and joining me at basin and staring me through the mirror.

"Did you find Agent Smith who tried to kill Rajni sir, you poor Mr Neo?" I asked rinsing my hands.

"I did watch Matrix and my favorite Rajini movies, but how come you are asking me about the characters?" Gowtham asked with his mouth open.

"I am being deprived of sleep since the time I have been with you because of you being a fucking agent and your constant rattling because of your sleep disorder. Did I complain about that?" I asked pretending to be serious when I noticed his puppy face with an expression as if found guilty of something. I turned towards the exit and he followed me quietly.

"Please zip up your pants, what you're wearing inside might become the talk of the day," I giggled and he reacted instantly only to find his pants already zipped.

"Bloody *dyaam* you are...rascala..." he screeched and I loped away.

It was a frosty evening and I was sitting on the terrace. I had no option as my room was on the terrace. I was well insulated in my black sweat shirt. It was the kind of weather where one should be in a room with the heater on and a packet of groundnuts to munch on. I was feeling bored and thought of getting my guitar and giving it a try. I had had it with me since my college days and had not gone beyond a couple of leads.

I had hardly played anything when I noticed someone repeatedly calling my name rather urgently. I could see it was Gowtham who had come running up to the third floor, exhausted, impatient to convey something that he had just discovered.

"I have great news for us!"

"What's that?" I tried to concentrate on playing my guitar. He immediately reacted. He snatched the guitar, grabbed a chair and sat on it.

"Man! You won't believe this, I just saw a bombshell and a cute girl on the second floor. I guess the girls have moved in and now we can find one..."

Before he could complete his sentence we were greeted by another soft voice.

"Hey! Hi!"

It was Eva. She came and greeted me, shook hands and smiled as if we were good friends.

"How was your day? How have you been? What are you doing here? I guess you must be having office ha, cool weather you know."

One statement and too many questions, and most self-answered.

I was just standing observing her; she was restless and didn't notice that Gowtham was staring at her with his mouth open. I smiled as she blabbered. Gowtham unknowingly ran his fingers on the guitar strings, only to produce an unpleasant sound that stopped her from jabbering and allowed me to introduce Gowtham to her.

She greeted him nicely, shook hands and left him awestruck. He held her hand firmly and she pulled it out giving him a weird look.

"It's nice that you play the guitar," she addressed Gowtham with a smile, complementing him. She insisted him to play a track and how could he say no when he was holding the guitar like a *sitar*.

"Thank you...but I play Tamil saangs, you will hardly understand that, so let him play a nice saang for you."

Pointing towards me, he handed me the guitar and left me in a situation where I could not say no to the bombshell who cutely added a long pleeeasseee.

Now what do you expect? In a movie, the guy out of the blue, with no knowledge of an instrument and pathetic vocals will suddenly start to sing the song of his life with the perfect lyrics. Snow will begin to fall and the girl will look like a fairy while the neighbours will join the chorus. Finally the guy with the shy smile on his face will win the heart of the woman. Bullshit!

I tried playing a few leads of Bollywood tracks which she could recognize. I fumbled with the rhythm but Gowtham seemed impressed because he hardly understood anything.

"I am just an amateur," I justified and my introvert gesture got a big thank you out of her and she half hugged me.

"I wish my boyfriend could play something for me," she said and complemented me as if I had discovered the rhythm she had lost somewhere. I was enjoying this; she was good but now she was even better. Gowtham started signaling at me and gave me an impish smile. I glared at him. I was wondering if I was too dumb or was she someone who liked little things? But I found her sweett. The guy problem! I told you I guess.

"Dumb!" she exclaimed, suddenly changing her expression from cheerful to remorseful. Did she reply to what I was thinking a second ago? Was I really dumb?

"My boyfriend is dumb, he doesn't even care," she stated and I felt relieved. It was addressed to someone else. I guess it was the third time she tried involving her boyfriend in our conversation and I couldn't resist asking about him. I guess it was a mistake.

It was a story that started at 10.00 p.m. Let me remind you it was a cold winter night, and we were on the terrace. It ended almost after half past eleven. Gowtham quit the gathering about forty-five minutes before the end when he received a call from his hometown. All the while I sat numb in the cold with my hands in my pockets. I was trying hard to not shiver in front of someone who apparently thought I was her best buddy! It seemed this beauty with no brain would make me skip dinner as well.

"I think we will break up soon; I am done with him. He is getting on my nerves. He was never like this. He is trying to curb my freedom," she lamented and expected me to say something. Meanwhile Gowtham joined us again. I would have advised her like any other guy, but due to the biting cold, I decided to give her genuine advice, though she was one of the options I was considering for myself.

"You should talk to him; the method you shared with me will work well if you share your thoughts with him. There is no point keeping things inside yourself and ending your relationship before hearing what he has to say," I said like a perfect teacher and noticed her paying attention. In between I noticed Gowtham trying hard to signal something. I guess he did not like my suggestion. Ignoring him, I continued.

"What if he is thinking the same about you? What if he wants to share the same with you? Convey your feelings but in a way you'd discuss stuff with your friends…every boyfriend is a friend first…" She cut me short.

"I do tell him but he doesn't listen, in fact he starts fighting with me" she expressed.

"Oh hell…*kodomay* baayfriend," Gowtham could not resist letting his emotion out.

I looked at him and he again gestured with his hands quickly pointing at her. I decided to ignore him.

"There is a difference between saying things bluntly and sharing things lightly. You might be sounding like a nag rather than being romantic or friendly. The last thing I would say is better put aside your relationship and sort out your friendship with him first."

I thought of putting an end to it, because that was it. I could hardly understand what I was saying myself. But she was serious and quiet. We expected her to say something, and finally after thirty seconds of dead silence, she reacted.

"I think you are right. It's been a long time since we have sat down for a few minutes and spoken to each other without fighting. We have forgotten our friendship. Thank you so much. See you guys. It's late now."

Saying this, she stood up, patted my back, winked at Gowtham and left.

"What the hell were you trying to tell me then?" I asked Gowtham while pacing towards our room. We entered, switched on the heater and had our dinner.

"Why were you giving her such pathetic advice?" Gowtham asked removing his specs only to get a shrug from me.

"Let them fight, they are a stupid couple. I wanted you to tell her to leave that rascala, and come to you…or better, to me," Gowtham said and I laughed at his straight and serious face.

"I wanted to suggest that as well. Who would not want to date a girl like her, but I don't know why I feel like a preacher when I dole out advice," I said winking at him.

"Pathetic, stupid fool you are. I guess she is interested in you. Look at the way she was staring at you while you were playing the guitar and while you were giving her worthless advice," he declared while clearing the plates after dinner.

"Dear Gowtham, if a girl is free with us doesn't mean she is interested, do you get that? She has a boyfriend and she doesn't seem to be the sort to cheat on him. Now please! Switch off the light," I ordered.

He switched off the lights and we both went to bed after the tiring day. He suggested before going into sleep-talk mode, "You wanted to find someone to have fun with, why do you mind if she has a boyfriend or not. Don't give suggestions, enjoy with the sexy girl. If you are not willing, then I am dozing off with her in my dreams. I will enjaaay. Good night." He giggled and went quiet.

He fell asleep in a flash and I was left thinking. Was she staring at me? What if she was interested in me? Not bad. I didn't want love or anything serious. But how could I date a girl who already had a boyfriend. Next time I won't give her any advice, I will ask her to break up with him, I thought. I am better and I can be a cool boyfriend. Wow! What a thought. I was enjoying the feeling. I smiled and quickly covered my face to get some sleep.

We got our seats allocated in the new office and finally work began. I was involved in the development profile where I was working on writing complex codes to develop a management system for the client. I was using Oracle, PL/SQL the languages that every average IT student would hate to deal with; he just wants a healthy package. I was least interested in writing codes and was more interested in other activities. One of them was writing and blogging, nothing meaningful though.

I started writing when I had a chat with my team lead. She was pretty, and I could not resist her smile and her words which always directed me to write multiple code lines to develop modules, completing the task assigned to me in my office and sometimes discussing the fundamentals of life. I was not her favorite but she was nice to talk to and was always supportive when anyone got stuck with anything. She was a fervent reader, a true fan of apt writing and very well read. She was Pallavi. She was smart, intelligent, and pragmatic, a touch emotional as well. I was not thinking anything about her, definitely not. But I enjoyed the feeling of making an impact on her, though I had tried impressing my manager as well, but failed.

I started to write blogs on some TG site which was developed with a concept to engage aspirants who would be sharing knowledge and data regarding the current topics, forums covered for MBA preparation and definitely blogging. They invited people to carve up, converse, remark and even acknowledge the creative writings of people who contributed. I would have never visited that site till I found Pallavi sitting and going through it. I found her commenting enthusiastically on some blog with the title *'Love never dies – it's the will'*. I couldn't resist asking her about it while reading her comment without her approval.

"I guess it's more or less a lame statement," I said to make her a little conscious and she pressed the submit button and turned towards me. She seemed keen to discuss it. Love is a topic about which everyone has something to proclaim. She replied not only with a smile, but contradicted my statement as well.

"Why do you feel this statement is negative? I guess the author is absolutely right."

She turned her revolving chair towards me and gestured to me to pull a chair and sit with her. As I pulled up the chair, I quickly recalled what I had said. I'd have to stick to my point. With a grin I took a second calculating my words before thoughtlessly blurting out the words like I had done before.

"Where there is *will*, there is love; and where there is love, the desire to make it happen never comes to a halt and in return the *will* never dies," I said with a smile.

"Nice statement! So you mean, even in case when someone does not attain his/her girl or boy, the will to achieve love never dies. If that's the case then people will never be able to move on in life and there will only be single stories, either of mere loneliness or victory."

She gave a credible reply which I acknowledged maintaining eye contact to notice the glow in her eyes. Lovely they were!

"Did I mention the desire to attain love or a person?' I asked smiling. She looked at me expecting me to elaborate what I had just said. I persisted.

"I apologize if I puzzled you. I mean the will to attain love never ends by losing a person; the desire to be loved or to give love is everlasting. A person is a body, love is a soul and will is the reason to live. Losing a person might mean loneliness, but searching and attaining love is victory."

The sheer tenderness in my voice made sure she was hooked to the conversation, to make her feel that she was still the superior one. But I don't know how I managed to give such a philosophical reply. It may have been her eyes that I was reading and reflecting. She was constantly looking into my eyes, thinking hard about what I had said. She raised her eyebrows and gave me a smile.

"Yes, true I guess, but then how come one still loves someone knowing that one can never be together with that someone," she asked innocently as if I had done my thesis on the subject called love. I didn't want to preach, so I decided to share with her a story which my communication skills teacher had shared with me during my college days. I didn't learn anything from it, but I thought that story was apt for this situation. I started as she looked at me attentively.

"There was a guy who fell in love with a girl as soon as she joined the tenth standard from another school. She was beautiful, and the guy was smart and genuine. As the days passed by, his love for her grew. He would keep making notes of what she wore, what she did and what she loved. It was a pure feeling, to experience the beauty called love. Each day, the will to attain his love began. Finally he made the effort and after a span of three years, he finally managed to propose to her the day after which he knew that they might not meet again or they would forever be together, as it was the last day of school. Unfortunately, he was rejected. He was devastated. Time kept its pace and four years were gone in a flash, and the desire to attain love and will was stronger than before. The will kept his hope alive and finally he found her in a different city where he proposed to her again, but the result was the same. He was crushed, ripped apart...but the aspiration to attain love did not waver. Fifteen years later, he found her again. She was happily married by then and had a little kid, but he followed her. He managed to locate her place and finally he rang the doorbell. The door opened and there was his beauty, as fresh as ever. He stared at her, couldn't believe that his quest of love had made him finally reach his destination. The *will* kept him alive and he proposed to her. She said yes and he attained the love that he had been searching for."

I paused and noticed the excitement in her eyes. She stated.

"Wow! Finally after fifteen years she said yes to him!"

She was delighted, as if she had seen the perfect ending, but then her expression changed and I noticed the little wave of doubt. She continued in an inquisitive tone, "How come she said yes when she was happily married with a kid? How can she disrupt her settled life?"

She caught me and I could see her seeking for a positive end. The guy should not be rejected and the girl's married life should not be disrupted. I pressed the start button, and began from where I had paused.

"Well, the girl who said yes to the guy was not the same girl; she was her sister and they were not twins."

I smiled and concluded to find an appalled look on her face. How cute she looked. I knew she must be thinking how could the guy propose to the sister and find love. So I continued.

"The quest here was to attain love; the *will* kept the hope alive not for the person, but for the love. So he rang the doorbell; the door opened and she was there to greet him. He stared at her, she looked intently at him. Time paused and both of them stood still, lost in the moment. Finally he found the love he was seeking for and she found him when he proposed." I finished and she nodded with a huge smile. Suddenly a shrill voice interrupted us.

"*Abe gadhe*, you are trying to mislead our team lead with your stupid jabbering," Chiya chuckled and Gowtham stood beside her.

I found him nodding in agreement. Chiya, Gowtham and I had developed a bond. We were more or less like buddies. I stood up and felt embarrassed, but I maintained a grin. I tried making fun of my own story to bring down the moment to a lighter note. Honestly, I had no idea if the story made sense or not, but I was feeling content of at least making an impression on Pallavi, with of course no other intentions. I was about to leave when Pallavi spoke after laughing at the conversation I was having with Chiya and Gowtham. It was friendly teasing and rather comical.

"You stuck to your point, no matter how illusory your story was. I must suggest that you write. This is a good site and you can find different people reading, commenting and suggesting on your work," she suggested pointing towards the website. The first article that I wrote was '*Love never dies, till the will is alive*'. When I wrote it, I sent the link to Pallavi, keeping everyone in CC, with a special note mentioning her. I clicked on the send button, winked at Gowtham who threw a folded paper napkin at me while Chiya ruffled my hair to tease me.

It was the weekend. I came to drop Gowtham to the metro station as he was going to spend the weekend at his uncle, *Shri Dakshinamoorthy Sawarpillayi's* place at Tagore Garden. I got late in office and was left with no option but to buy some chips and a chocolate for dinner.

I reached home late after giving Rajshree aunty a call to give me the keys to open the gate which they usually closed by 11.00 p.m. I let out a sigh of relief after reaching the room as it had started to drizzle by then. After freshening up, I comforted myself in the warmth of the quilt when there was a knock at the door. It was tough getting out as I had just opened the packet of wafers. When the knocking continued, I had to get up. It was Eva, to my surprise. She was in her cardigan that seemed to be the only garment providing warmth and rest was too revealing in the frightening cold weather. She wore navy blue shorts with a light grey loose top. Her flowing hair was open , a hint of kohl around her eyes.

"Can I come in?" she asked tilting her neck sideways, flashing a sticky smile. I still could not believe that it was her. It was midnight after all. Before I could say yes or even nod, she pushed past me. One thing I desperately wanted to ask her, 'Don't you feel cold Eva?'

"Wow! Nice cozy room" she expressed as she removed her pink slippers. She picked up the chocolate kept and slipped into the quilt while I was still holding the door. I was stunned. It happened so quickly that I had no idea what to do. A sexy girl entering the room and without you even putting any effort, getting into your bed – it was a dream come true.

"Why are you standing there? It's your place, you can also sit here. It's freezing cold, so please shut the door," she stated and ripped apart the chocolate wrapper. Before I could follow her orders and shut the door to make myself comfortable under the same quilt, I saw that only the last two slabs of chocolate were left, which she offered to me. She then pounced on the packet of wafers kept nearby. It was embarrassing for me to tell her that it was my dinner. To save the remaining bit of my dinner, I smartly removed the packet of chips from her vision and hid it under the bed. It sounds cheap but I was hungry and I couldn't bear to sleep hungry. I was sure that she didn't notice that as she was busy consuming the wafers and blabbering about something, all I understood was that she hadn't had dinner because she had a fight with her boyfriend, and she promised him that she would not eat anything till he comes and apologizes. How well she was keeping the promise!

"I hope there won't be a problem if the Doctor Lady comes to know that you are in my room," I said while safely removing the packet out of her sight and slipping it under the head side of my bed.

"Don't worry, she sleeps by ten every day, and Rajshree will never come to this floor at this time, so chill!"

She had finished the wafers but still looked hungry. She couldn't find anything else so I was the only medium left in the room to concentrate on. She started narrating her story and I came to know that the reason for the recent fight was her late hours and the fact that she travels alone, sometimes at even two or three in the morning. Well, the guy's point seemed justified and he was just caring.

"But that's nice of him; I guess he is right. It's not safe in Delhi and..." I said supporting him. I never wanted to support the boyfriend. I reminded myself of Gowtham's words that I should go against her boyfriend so that I could woo the hot lady, but I had stated otherwise. I promised myself that I will not give her any advice. Instead, I will try to win her as my girlfriend. Quick thought!

"Why is he right?" she interrupted my thoughts and began an oration on girl power and the fact that girls can do whatever they wanted. It's modern India and girls have equal rights and so on. She gave a ten minute long speech on woman prowess while I nodded. I had no energy to support what was obvious.

"And excuse me, you should not support him; my boyfriend hates you," she suddenly turned to me. So now I had an enemy whose girlfriend was sharing her stories with me.

"Why? What have I done? I haven't even seen him," I said with raised eyebrows.

"Don't worry, he won't harm you. I told him that there is a guy staying on the third floor, but he is not good looking," she chuckled. "So that he doesn't feel I can be interested in you and…" she paused after hurting my ego with the 'not good looking' comment. I frowned.

What do you mean by not-good-looking? I wanted to ask her. Of course I was an average looking guy, but that doesn't mean she should say that to my face. But I wanted to hear the next part and asked her to continue.

"Can I have some water please?" she asked in between. I quickly ran towards the shelf to get a water bottle and gave it to her in a second. She drank some and continued.

"The worst part is that he saw you yesterday and enquired about you. He said that you are a fine looking guy so why did I lie to him. He asked me to stay away from you." She stated and gulped the remaining water in my bottle. Now even the water was gone. Looks like I would have to go thirsty as well that night!

"Wow! That's good; he seems to be a nice guy. At least he found me fine looking unlike you," I stated calmly with a smile, regaining my pride about my looks.

"Ya re! I just said that because I didn't want him to enquire too much about you, else he would ask me to shift," she expressed in a sad tone.

I remained quiet but then quickly asked her a question. In case I decided to start my plan of snatching her away from her boyfriend, I should at least know what that guy does.

"He is a gym trainer," she said not looking at me.

"You mean weight lifter… aa… I mean he must be lifting weights and must have a well built body!" I asked as I pictured a bouncer in my mind.

"Yes he is, and you know he is so possessive about me that he has thrashed a few guys recently just because they were staring at me. *Aise thodi hota hai.* It doesn't work like that."

I was numb. I wasn't even feeling cold anymore. I was thinking I could be added to the list of thrashed guys. I was not only staring at her, I was talking to his girl. I was planning to hit on her and the worst part was that she was sitting under my quilt, my feet almost rubbing against hers! Wonderful! She continued.

"You must be careful, avoid using this lane."

She pointed to a random direction and showed concern for me. I recalled what she had said a minute ago that he wouldn't harm me. That was in contrast to her last statement. Was she trying to help me or make me panic? She went back to the topic of women and freedom. But there was a dip in my excitement about her. I was less attentive and hardly paid any attention towards the girl till I found her moving closer to me, pressing her feet against mine. She held my hand in hers and took me into a different world where I kind of lost my senses.

"Do you think I am that bad?" she asked moving her face close to mine. A soft whispering tone, the question was out of context, but her tone was tender, a soft emotion, a clear void but not desperation that she was unable to express despite expressing everything. It happened so suddenly that I was confused what it was all about and in contrast to the conversation a minute ago.

"No Eva...yyou are good...vvery nice... Why?" I asked making a nervy eye contact and then asked her the reason of her sudden inquisitiveness to know about her. I was stammering and couldn't move.

"Then why does that bastard want to kiss another girl? Even I want to kiss someone else," she said and before I knew what was going on, she quickly moved herself almost on top of me. She was on her knees holding my hands tightly and there was a gap between us. I could smell her fragrance which was as good as she was looking in her loose grey top. A red bra strap could be seen under her top. Her cardigan was unbuttoned and she placed my left hand on her smooth waist. Her hair fell over me, covering my face, her eyes looking into mine. But they were a little moist and I wondered if it was due to guilt of what she was doing or her emotions for me.

A thousand thoughts were running in my mind. What if her boyfriend comes to know about this? What if he just makes a filmy entry banging on the door and shouting at us? Why is she behaving like that? Then I recalled poor Gowtham's advice of forgetting everything else and going for the kill, or the kiss in this case. Shall I hold her more gently to give her a sense of affection that one gets when in love or in a relationship? Shall I move an inch closer and seal the gap between us to give her the comfort and desire she is searching for? Shall I hug her tightly and press her securely against me? Shall I start to feel her body with my shivering fingers and nervous hands? Her eyes were closed, she relaxed her body against mine. I could sense her softness against my chest. She was breathing faster, and releasing my hand, she placed her left hand softly around my neck. She was on my body now. It was tough controlling myself when she was expecting me to lock lips. I wanted to, but I guess I was feeling like a mere object which she was using to satisfy her ego because she was hurt by her love who just kissed someone else or might be thinking of kissing someone else. Had it not been the case I would have gone for the kiss, but my lips were quivering, I couldn't stop her and her lips almost touched mine when we felt something between our thighs. Something was vibrating and she abruptly opened her eyes. They opened wide and she cried,

"Oh my god! My boyfriend must be calling."

She immediately got up, hurting my thighs hard with her strong knees. I was looking at her with a big question mark and she continued, "I have to run to my room. He often gets suspicious that I might be in your room and will ask me to give the phone to my roommate to confirm. But you don't sleep; I am coming in ten minutes after the call," she ordered or requested, I failed to understand, but while wearing her slippers she noticed the packet of chips which I had hidden. She quickly grabbed that, thanked me for the snacks and kissed me on the cheeks. She was gone in a flash.

I remained still for at least five minutes; it was like everything had happened in a jiffy. Shall I regret that I missed a chance of getting cozy with a girl who just wanted to quench her desire after being hurt by her so called boyfriend? Shall I curse the guy who called at the wrong time? If I stop being selfish and stop contemplating on the thought of time pass, the thing which was fluttering in my mind was the sudden manner in which she had presented herself. The only conclusion was that either she was hurt that she couldn't take the thought of being cheated on, or she was done with his possessiveness. Where there is a relation, there must be love. Where was the love?

Though I missed an opportunity that every guy seeks, but the moment didn't demand the act or I was a fool for not grabbing it. I was lost in my thoughts and hungry as well. She had eaten my food as well as my peace of mind. If there would have been love, she wouldn't have been hurt; if she was hurt, then there must be the ego that didn't get footing to root itself on the ground. Oh cool! I was thinking in line with Shikha's thoughts, the girl I had met in the train. This was an apt example of love meeting ego. I hope she meant the same.

The Futile Team Meetings

The eve of Lohri was around the corner and we were awaiting a holiday the next day as government offices were closed. To get such holidays was exciting because we were working with our client. It was a usual working day at the MNC. Chiya, Gowtham and I had prepared an itinerary for the day. Our virtual plan didn't last long when we received a mail from our manager Mr. Teja stating that we wouldn't be granted a holiday. The ten members were adamant that they wouldn't come to office and were ready to reject the mail sent by Mr. Teja. The fear in our minds was: 'how could we go against his order?' Each member of the team began to come up with the worst possible ideas.

"*Hum to beemar hai, hum kehdenge,*" Chiya bagged the safest reason one could have used, that she will fall sick.

"I will say that my landlady's dog bit me, that scoundrel Scooby," Gowtham giggled and patted himself for what he thought was a brilliant idea.

"As if he will not ask you to get the doctor's prescription," I said getting him to think of some other idea.

"Then I will say that Scooby bit you and I had to take you to the doctor," he giggled again to feel self appraised only to get a glare from me.

"See we will convince him. Chiya will be our spokesperson, and I guess everybody is in," I said.

Chiya was the best person as she had made a good impression on the manager. Everyone nodded in agreement, but Chiya had different thoughts.

"Why should I lead? I'd rather stick to my idea to get sick that very day rather than convince him for the non-existent holiday," she said and shook her head. In the end, we turned towards the other team members but nobody was willing to bell the cat. I could hear the enthusiasm in Gowtham's voice when he took charge asking everybody to go and convince our manager. We all were sitting in the conference room away from the government officials. It seemed we were having an important discussion. Finally Gowtham stood up in half a rage and began to speak like a true speaker.

"If no one is willing to take the responsibility, then I will go to that guy and convince him. I am not scared like you people are. Blaady scary crows."

'Scary crows? Are you sure you want to say scary crows?' I questioned with not so soothing expressions to the unfitted title he had just conferred on all of us.

"That's not funny," he stated with authority. No one laughed. I was finding it tough to control myself. I did not look at him as I could have burst into laughter seeing his Hitler-like expressions.

"That's final, Gowtham will take on the daunting task of convincing him," I announced, pretending to bite my nails and covering my face. I gave a mischievous smile as I glanced at Gowtham walking out proudly and banging the door behind him. We laughed our hearts out for the next few minutes.

So as per the plan, we all were ready after the serious conference we had had. Gowtham's seat was next to our manager's location, so as soon as Mr. Teja arrived, we would get a signal from him. I'd be like a vice-captain following Gowtham who would start the conversation. Everything went as per plan. Our manager came in, set up his laptop and began working immediately, without noticing that Gowtham was standing an inch behind him, followed by me and then by the rest of the team. Gowtham was standing quietly behind him, waiting for him to notice him on his own. We stood behind him silently looking at each other, fearing his reaction. The government officials who were working along with us were watching us inquisitively.

"Will you ask him now?" I whispered startling Gowtham who seemed to have become a dummy.

"Oh shut up! I will, can't you see he is busy?" he hissed angrily.

"But we can't keep standing like this, you'll have to call him… Excuse..." Before I could say anything else we found Mr. Teja shuffling in his seat and turning towards his right. Gowtham immediately settled himself on his seat which was on the left side of our manager, leaving me exposed with a half-compiled sentence stuck in my mouth.

"Excuse me, sir."

"Yes. Do you want anything?" Mr. Teja asked calmly rotating his chair in my direction.

"Yes, aa…all of us wanted to ask you about the holiday?' I pointed behind me. He moved his head a bit to check who was standing behind and then stared at me for a while and asked, "We? Who else is with you?"

"Yes sir! The whole team is there and..." I said and turned my head to check what was obvious. They had all disappeared Bloody *scary crows!* No one was there. I could see everyone well settled in their respective seats, pretending to be busy, as if they were least bothered about what were we up to. I had been ditched and left like a prey in front of a wolf.

"So you wanted to discuss the Lohri holiday which I have already mailed you about. I clearly stated that you people have to follow your MNC calendar. Did you find any ambiguity while reading that?" he asked staring straight at me.

"Aa...no...the team had planned and we thought that if we could...aa...aa...enjoy our Lohri holiday," I stammered stressing on the words 'team' and 'we'.

He sighed and said in an irked tone, "I guess there is no team and you are alone. If you want a special holiday, then finish your work for today, work the whole night and apply for leave."

I was convinced that there was no point in trying to convince him. I guess the government officials who were watching us saw how strict the manager was, as well as the MNC's rules. Mr. Teja got up from his seat and stood a few inches away from me. The heavy built man made me a little more nervous and scared, but I pretended to be calm and submissive.

"No worries, sir, I must take your leave. I need to finish my work," I said as cool as a cucumber. I turned back to leave and noticed my teammates staring at me. It was an amusement, a set of giggles that might erupt anytime.

"Wait! Tell me, are you kind of a minister who will lead the team to sudden victory? Oh bhai, *neta hai tu?*" he tried to be funny with that sarcastic remark. I was still wondering what to do next but could only give a fake smile.

"No sir! Nothing like that, I must leave," I said and glancing at Gowtham, who was staring me at me and chortling. I felt like punching him, but his giggling made me smile.

"Why are you smiling?" my manager asked suddenly.

"Nothing, sir," I said before walking away.

"Weird guy," he said and sat down on his seat. I am damn sure if he would have left the room at that time, the whole team would have laughed. I sat on my seat pretending to be serious about my work and unmoved for at least the next four hours.

It had already become one of my important work agendas to write something on that blogging site. I have to be honest, I wasn't passionate about writing, but it was all for one faithful reader in the beauty called Pallavi. One critic who always found irrelevant faults in my writing was Chiya. Gowtham was my neutral reader. He would only comment 'I agree with both' while filling up the comment section. Whereas Pallavi would initiate a discussion, Chiya would only disapprove. Each time after commenting, she would ping me to check her comment, only to give me a thumbs down with a mischievous smile while sharing a hi-five with Gowtham.

I noticed, however, that there was one reader who would always comment 'nice thought' or something motivating, specifically in my favour. She was an anonymous reader and one who was constantly following my posts. She had posted the comment under the name 'Contemporary brat'. It was a really weird username. I was more than happy to ignore her till she once posted, 'You are learning fast'. I could not see her face as her profile picture only showed kohl-rimmed black eyes. Very attractive though, and honestly, they didn't remind me of anyone. Though working as project engineer with enough coding work, I still managed to get time for all this nuisance or technically *'sidi siyapas'*. I started searching for her; it was tough because I was not on Facebook, by choice. I really got inquisitive to know more about her. I read close to fifty articles in her blog from which I concluded that she was as bold as her username. She didn't seem to be a spoiled brat as her blogs always ended in favor of respect towards the Indian culture. The genuineness of her words was apparent, but at the same time they were crafty enough to highlight an open thought and the fact which we all know and are unwilling to talk about. Her statements were enough to give one an adrenaline rush. The bold, black comedy, and seductive content in her blogs always dragged enough users who would write anything to impress her. A few girls criticized her, but the boys were mad enough to post their mobile numbers in the comment section. Some titles of her articles in her blog included '*Seducing is an art*' or '*A key with many holes around*', '*Passion of the last night*', '*Drink and drive her*' and many more. Gosh! They were intrepid, audacious and the writing was such that you would think twice before arguing with her. She treaded upon many, and open fired people who tried criticizing her blog. She seemed to be a girl with an open mind, but hard to be convinced. All I could make out through her blog and comments was that I couldn't comment or chat with her; she would just murder me. It seemed that I was just a kid in the world where people were writing and fighting using words, vocabulary and thoughts rooted deep within their minds, as against which my writing was simple and lighthearted. After almost two days of going through her blog and writing, I was able to find her email id. I feared that she might say something which would be hard to digest if I commented on her blog, so I preferred mailing her.

Dear Contemporary Brat,

It feels great when you greet someone with a comment. It shows that what I am writing is not crap. I would love to thank you for giving your valuable time and appreciation. Don't know what your name is, but all I can see is that you have got enigmatic eyes and you write well. Pretty thoughtful!

Regards,

Amateur

The Wrong Cases

We were running late as we had decided to get off at Rajiv Chowk after office. We planned to meet, roam around and later have dinner. I came out of office asking Gowtham to hurry up as though we were going to have an important meeting.

"Oh man! Why are you running? Is there any *haat* chick waiting for you," Gowtham giggled in his signature style.

"Why are your expressions always in contrast to your statement? Change them!" I said walking briskly staring and smiling at him.

"That is the trick, you dumb ass. You know I am really good at changing expressions. Didn't you see for yourself when we went to talk to our manager last week regarding the holiday," he said teasing me and I lunged towards him to kick him. He was well prepared for my reaction. He immediately took a U-turn and started running towards the metro station. He crossed the road next to V3S Mall towards the juice corner as I chased him. Before I could catch him, we heard a lady.

"Thief! Thief! Please help me someone," she extended her right arm, made me stop at once and before I could understand what was happening, she pulled me towards her holding my arm and asked, "Do you have a cell phone? I want to make a call," she asked and started crying.

Meanwhile, since Gowtham had already been running, he feared of being caught and thrashed by the public if they thought him to be the thief. He tried hiding himself a few meters away from the scene. I had no intention to help her instead, I was suspicious. She may try to trick me and steal my phone. Nevertheless, I was confident of catching her as my legs were in good shape. All these thoughts ran in my mind alternatively. I was giving her my phone. She immediately dialed a number. I guess it was her husband.

"Rohan! I have lost my wallet; somebody in the bus stole it from my purse. All my cards were in it. What should I do?" she sobbed.

She was in a formal dress: a cream coloured shirt, a light yellow sweater with light grey pants. Might be working as a receptionist, because her dress was not that elegant; her command over language was also not that great. The local brown leather purse and lady's handkerchief of faded blue color clenched in her left hand were enough to convince me that she was a typical middle class earning house wife, a little less educated but determined to fight against the odds to match equally in supporting her husband to run her family.

A piece of advice came from the other end and she gave me my phone back. I was well aware of what had happened, but she thanked me for the phone and narrated the whole incident. The regret on her face was loud and clear. Gowtham was watching and slowly joined me when he saw that people had lost interest in the episode. I came to know that she had lost her wallet, which not only had a thousand bucks but a debit card. It was clear that we would have to help her in deactivating that card by calling her bank's customer care. Gowtham started dialing the customer care number and when he reached a level where one is supposed to enter the customer id or phone banking pin or at least an account number, we discovered that the lady didn't have the requisite information. She was so worried that she asked me to accompany her to her place where she would provide me with the details. I tried to say no, but before I could, she said with teary eyes, "No bhaiya, please! Can you come with me and help me, else my money will be gone," she pleaded.

I looked at Gowtham with a baffled expression, and before Gowtham could decipher my puzzled expressions, she interrupted with flowing tears. I was still in a dilemma; it could well turn out to be a case of fraud as I recalled the incidents I had heard in Delhi. She seemed genuine though. One can't be that good at acting or at least not in such a crowded place. These were the thoughts in my mind; I was trying to convince myself. Before I could decide what to do, she shouted for a cycle rickshaw.

"*Kaha chalengi, bibi ji?*" the rickshaw puller asked without looking at me.

"Geeta Colony road, near Narayan Mandir *jana hai*, *kitna loge*?"

He quoted his price and she climbed into the rickshaw and looked at me. I did the same and sat with her. Gowtham called me on the way and I spoke to him causally, trying to encrypt my sentences for him to decode. The lady sitting next to me was hardly paying any attention, but I still tried to be a man on an undisclosed mission, indicating my friend of handling things if per chance I fail to fall under prescribed time. To my bad, it was Gowtham at the other end, who hardly got anything, instead he thought that I might be pouncing a chance that I got to go with the young lady.

"Where are you going with the lady? She asked you and you didn't even look at me," Gowtham complained.

"Haha… Nothing like that, Charlie! It's just another project I will be taking care of. Right now, I will be going to Geeta Colony. I will be back in fifteen minutes. If not, then do call me again, buddy." I said pretending to be cool. I was acting like a secret agent. I tried looking at her, but saw that she looked worried and was looking at the other end of the road.

"Ohh! I got you. Another project! You just jumped on the opportunity. Going with Geeta…" he said giggling and completely misunderstanding me.

"No, you stupid! The place… her place... I mean her address is Geeta Colon…" I tried to clarify.

"Man you've hit jackpot. You going to Geeta's place? Enjay enjay…but why only fifteen minutes? Take your time, you filthy rascala. Bye," he chuckled as he disconnected the call.

"Wait Charliee... Gowtham… Stupid man!" I tried muttering his name without her hearing, but all in vain. What will happen next? What if she is an agent who befuddles strangers and take them to a place where her gang tortures them? What if I get kidnapped? I was wondering if I'd be taken to a distant place when the rickshaw puller took a left turn from the main road into a narrow lane, which seemed one of the busiest and nosiest streets of Delhi. She asked him to stop as the way was blocked by three Bajaj Chetaks standing in line behind a Maruti 800 cornered against the wall of a house with two general store shops in front of it. It was her house. The main door was open as her in-laws were shouting at someone. That someone turned out to be her.

"Stop it, Mama! He is not my friend. I have lost my purse and he is here to help me," she shouted at the top of her voice.

She ran inside and I kind of stood in between the entrance and the street. Her in-laws were staring at me suspiciously and paid no heed to my namaste. I was scared and wanted to run away. I started taking a step back and gestured to the rickshaw puller to turn in the other direction, but as soon as I gathered courage to move, the lady called me and came running towards me with all the documents. I looked at the bank details and finally we managed to lodge the request for cancelling her card. She insisted I come in and have some tea. I could see everyone still looking at me as though I had pretended to help her but was indeed her lover. I didn't take my time to say goodbye. I hurriedly made a u-turn and jumped onto the rickshaw. I could see her in-laws still cursing her while we peddled away. She screamed from behind and came running.

She stopped the rickshaw and said, "*Aap thoda baith kar jaate,*" she said in an apologetic tone. I told her my name and gave her my number as she had requested. I finally saw a smile on her face as she waved me goodbye.

Since he thought I was with Geeta, Gowtham went to Rajiv Chowk alone. It was late when Gowtham entered through the gate at ten. He hurried as he apologized to Rajshree aunty. He was fine till he reached the first floor where he heard the owner's beagle barking. He heard the sound clearly as though the dog was especially waiting for him. He stopped and stood as still as a statue. He waited for him to calm down and allow him to pass. I was unaware that he would be coming home this late. I was almost about to doze off when I received a call from Gowtham.

"Hello! I can't talk, read my message, you asshole," he commanded in a whispering tone and hung up, forcing me to check my messages. There were about twenty messages from him the likes of which were 'save me', 'bloody *dyam* will bite me', 'lady's dog blocking my way' and so on. The twentieth message was full of rage. I wore my slippers and went down. I found him drenched in sweat, stuck by the staircase.

"Why are you stuck here?" I asked the obvious question to which I already had the answer.

"Shhh... Please check if the dog is gone," he said looking out fearfully.

"He must be sleeping inside?" I growled at him. I went close to him and forced him to come upstairs. He was reluctant, but I didn't leave him with a choice. We were almost about to cross the lady doctor's room door and I suggested to him to check whether the dog was sleeping by putting his ear against the door. We were facing each other, almost resting our hands on the knees, bending half. I could still see the fear in his eyes through his glasses though it was dark.

"Are you happy now? That lady and *daag* are in deep sleep. Grow up man!" I lashed at him.

"Ya man! But how would I know. I didn't come upstairs."

I thumped my forehead in frustration.

"Arrrhh...shut up. Let's move now."

Before we could stand up, straight, we heard the door knob turn. The lights were switched on and before we could understand what was happening, we saw a giant figure standing almost parallel to us. It was our landlady, who had caught us in an awkward position...peeping into her door.

"What are you guys doing here?" she asked with authority as if she had caught a couple of thieves. Meanwhile, we stood upright like two soldiers in front of a colonel.

Gowtham muttered, "Ohh man... haarible..."

Just then, the lady's beagle started barking, as if wanting us to be handed over to him.

I tried to control the situation by saying, "He was scared of Scooby, so..."

"So you guys were trying to peep through the door to check whether he is alive or dead?" She interrupted me sternly while Gowtham tried to hide behind me.

"No...no..." I tried to explain. "I was trying to show him how Scooby can sense us...and how we can befriend him."

I could hardly understand what I had said.

"You were trying to befriend a dog at midnight? Through a keyhole?" she asked sternly.

Gowtham finally gathered courage to butt in, "No doctor! I thought you have kept your daag out. I was stuck here for half an hour when my friend came and saved me from the naai.

"Naai?" she said looking confused.

I clarified, "He means daag...dog...Scooby!"

"Whatever it is, please go and sleep. It's late now. Don't be scared of Scooby and don't peep next time." She stormed off as we made our escape.

NIC office:

It was almost a week since I had mailed Contemporary Brat. I had forgotten all about her till I received an email from her.

> *Dear Amateur,*
>
> *Thanks for the compliments, but don't even think that you can try your luck on me. Oops! I must be scaring you. Well just kidding! Like the way you write and that's why spend time reading it. But a lot of things to work upon, and well...you are learning.*
>
> *Contemporary Brat*

I liked the way she responded. It was similar to the style to her blogs, dynamic and something that would keep one on his or her toes. I wanted to know more, at least wanted her to type more.

I was in a dilemma whether to end the conversation or carry on. Honestly, I wanted to ask her more and know about her. I couldn't resist and mailed her. It took at least half an hour to press the send button though. I was thinking about her reply when I got a call.

"Hello bhaiya! Do you recognize me? Jaya here."

A very soft voice greeted me. It was the same lady I had helped the other day.

"Hi! How're you? Hope you are fine and you have managed to save your money as well," I replied trying to be witty.

"Yes yes! I am very happy that I met you at the right time, thank you so much bhaiya," she said in excitement. I put my phone an inch away from my ear after I heard the word '*bhaiya*' even though I had no untoward intentions towards the lady. She was almost shouting in excitement and her voice was filled with gratitude, but I was least interested. I suddenly heard something which caught my attention.

"...and you know I shared my story with one of my best friends Aridhita. She wants to talk to you now," she said in a go. I was alert now, adjusting my chair while paying attention to the new voice that had just greeted me.

"Hi, how're you? Good to know that people like you exist in this world. People who go out of their way to help others," she stated. Her voice was pleasant and she was better at conversing in comparison to Jaya who sounded crass.

I was thinking of an old saying like '*mera farz tha*' but that would have been too formal and old fashioned. In return,

I acknowledged her compliment, smiled and asked formal questions to know a little more about her. I guess if I remember correctly, we spoke for almost an hour. I didn't even realize when I left my seat and went downstairs. We hung up only when Jaya taunted her playfully about me. I can imagine how fast that was going on. I came to know a lot about her. She told me how she had met Jaya, how often she goes to her place, how and where they both spend time and so on. And the best part was that she was working in the building next to Scope Minar as a consultant in some private firm. I could understand how good she must be at consulting, for she sure knew how to talk! We ended our conversation after agreeing to catch up soon. She returned the phone to her friend.

"Bhaiya, what's going on ha? She is my sweetest friend. You both seem to have forgotten me… Bad haa," she said teasing us like a typical college-going student. I just smiled and we hung up finally. Well! That was it and I was excited. I was trying to take it casually but this seemed to be karma. I had helped someone unintentionally and now it seemed the favour was being returned. I was looking forward to the meeting with Aridhita. I went over to share my story with Gowtham.

"Aah! Oh man! You spent fifteen minutes with Geeta and got her friend Aditya as well," Gowtham stared at me with eyes wide open in disbelief.

"Her name is Aridhita, not Aditya, damn it. She is a girl, and that lady's name is not Geeta. She is Jaya whom I helped and not made out with. Correct your stats, you ill-minded asshole!" I hissed at him and gulped juice while he was still holding his glass, taking long sips. After a few minutes of staring at me blankly, he nodded in agreement to what I had said.

"Ooh, now what will you do? You will do time pass with Jaya or Aradhita?" he asked. I punched him hard on the back.

"Aah…that hurt. Oh look there, that bastard punched her," he stated pointing in the opposite direction. I didn't look as I was sure he was playing a prank.

"Oh god! That rascala punched Eva," Gowtham said getting agitated. As soon as I heard the name Eva, I turned and saw the final blow to her face. It was a tight slap. Before we could react, we saw Eva running towards the flat. They were some distance away from us. I shouted hard at her by calling her name, but she didn't hear us. We ran towards the flat while her boyfriend ran in the opposite direction. He must have seen us shouting. Though it was a quarter to ten, there were many people out on the road. We quickly entered our building looking for Eva, even though we were not allowed to enter the second floor where girls were staying. I went inside while Gowtham chose the safer option of signaling me if anyone came enquiring. There were four rooms. Two locked and one was a kitchen. There was one room where the light was on. It must be Eva's. I knocked at the door and she opened it after ten minutes. I already had a vision of breaking open the door to find her hanging from the ceiling fan!

"Are you fine?" I said without even letting her open the door completely.

"Yes, I am fine. What happened?" she said pretending to be fine but her face was wet with tears. She was in a tight white shirt that reached her thighs. God she was hot. I didn't look anywhere else except into her eyes. I felt sorry for her. I looked at her for a few seconds. Leaving her alone would be a better option, so I concluded with a few consoling lines.

"Don't worry, things will be fine…" I had hardly begun the sentence when she threw herself at me. She hugged me tightly and cried like a child. I was stunned. I feared Rajshree aunty or the landlady arriving at the scene to find me standing at the edge of the girl's door hugging her. No one would believe my honest intentions; a cup of milk at the beer bar is bound to be considered as alcohol. While she was sobbing, I saw Gowtham who was standing still like a statue staring at me hugging Eva. When he noticed that I was looking at him, he winked at me and showed me a thumbs up sign and left.

No no Gowtham, you dumb fool. This is not what I meant. I tried to convey my thoughts to him. Eva was crying. She didn't let me go and instead clutched my collar with her right hand which had curled around my neck. Her fragrance was more than attractive. I wasn't hugging her and my hands were still off, just resting on her for the sake of support. I was sweating as I was nervous. I whispered to her, "Eva, I think I should leave. If I get caught, I will be thrown out and you will be in a mess, sweetheart."

I don't know why I called her 'sweetheart', but I was in a flow. I just wanted her to loosen her grip so that I could run away.

"Please wait for a while. I need you. I am scared. At least wait till my roommate comes," she pleaded.

Releasing me from the never ending hug, she pulled me inside and shut the door. She remained an inch away, still holding my hand firmly. It would be a lie to say that I was not excited. It was a cozy girls' room. It was lit up with a dim light. Girly things were lying here and there. A hot girl stood just a millimetre away, breathing heavily, and as always showing her voluptuous figure, but I was scared and nervous too. She began to tell me about her relationship with this guy who had started putting a noose around her freedom, her rights and her clothes. He wasn't like that when she met him; he used to be the perfect guy who would take care of her, listen to her, and bear her tantrums. Then why had he changed suddenly? How could he betray her and sleep around with her best friend?

I listened quietly to her. Maintaining a cautious distance from her, I just repeated my words.

"Don't worry. Things will be fine."

She moved an inch closer, clutched my right hand firmly in her left hand, and with her right hand, took my left hand and placed it gently on her waist. She closed her eyes, came closer and kissed me. The kiss was fiery rather than smooth, and happened in anger rather than any other feeling. I guess it was just to stamp an authority, maybe proving to her inner conscious that yes, I can kiss! I can kiss a random guy, she must have thought. If my boyfriend can, then I can as well. The kiss lasted for a few seconds. It definitely ended in guilt for her. She released me from her grip and didn't look at me. I could not say anything and decided to leave. I knew she wouldn't be in a mood to listen to me, nor would I be in a situation to explain myself. I left hurriedly. Much to my horror, I banged straight into Rajshree aunty.

"What are you doing here? Wasn't it clear that you boys are not allowed on this floor?" she questioned me sternly.

"Aa...I was looking for Gowtham. I thought he might have come here as he is scared of Scooby...so...," I faltered.

I could see Eva peeping out as Rajshree aunty raised her voice. Eva came out to support me and gave her a pretty solid reason for my presence. She assisted her to her room, and gave me an *'i-am-watching-you'* kind of look. I gave a sigh of relief and ran away.

I reached my room where Gowtham was waiting for me to get all the details. I was feeling low though. It wasn't that

I was beginning to have feelings for Eva. I knew that she had kissed me only to get back at her boyfriend and I was thinking in terms of half relationships. How will the guy feel when he gets to know that she kissed me? But he was already sleeping around, so she did right. But was I there to just support the cause? I was merely filling a void in her life at the moment.

"Ooh man! Tell what you did? What happened?" Gowtham asked interrupting my random thoughts. He was as excited as a reporter quizzing a minister caught in a scandal.

"Oh Gowtham, please! I didn't do anything. I was just trying to help her out," I said without looking at him.

"The kind of help you gave her would be envied by all men. They will compete hard to win a position to assist her," Gowtham chuckled.

He made me giggle, but I managed to control myself. I made a sad face. That made him serious and we discussed Eva and the aggressive guy who had slapped her in a public place. It was late when the discussion ended and before I could doze off, my phone beeped.

Hi, li'l late in dropping you this text. Hope you don't mind. Sleep well.

Your new friend

Aridhita

My sleepiness vanished as I read the message. Why would I mind her texting me? I replied quickly. So numbers were exchanged and a meeting was fixed for the next day. Of course she planned to come with Jaya, her best friend. Her message immediately took me to a new world, giving me a ray of hope.

There could be someone who might be there for me without any conditions, I thought, even though it was going to be our first meeting. Just count it as the first day excitement. Gowtham noticed my expressions, moved a little closer and peeped at the screen of my phone.

He read the message and said, "I hope this time you will stay on track. Don't fall in love. Remember this is only time pass," he winked as he switched off the lights.

How can I think of time pass when I have not seen her? But her voice was pretty attractive. If the text message had been written by hand I could have drawn some conclusions about her by the handwriting, but unfortunately, it was in Arial font. What rubbish was I thinking! One thing was for sure though – I was pretty excited about meeting her.

I was suddenly interrupted by loud snoring. I kicked Gowtham in exasperation.

"Why can't you sleep peacefully? Either you snore or you talk in your sleep! How can I sleep?" I shouted only to get a blank stare from him. Within seconds, he dozed off again.

I thought about both Eva and Aridhita. One whose story I knew well, and the other whom I'd get to know the next day.

Meeting Aridhita

"I hope she will be as nice as our Tirupur *nariyal malaii*," Gowtham giggled describing Aridhita while we were waiting near Mc Donald's at V3S Mall.

I didn't want to face them alone so I took Gowtham along. He was more than happy to accompany me. In return, he just wanted me to write a letter for him. An email, in fact, which he wanted to send to a girl he liked in our office. He had done his homework of getting all the information about the girl. I was happy till the point he told me her name was Jaspreet Kaur. She was a Sikh girl from Patiala who was in the NIC office working for the client. Gowtham found her sweet. He was a firm non-believer in caste or religion. I however imagined the innocent boy from Tirupur getting beaten up by the girl's family and had a vision of Gowtham shouting *'Maai Tirupur, maai Tamil, maai country'*. I smiled when he kicked me.

"Why are you smiling?"

"Have you ever been beaten up by the public or a group of people?" I asked with a straight face.

"No...why?" he asked with a frown.

"Because I was just imagining Jaspreet Kaur's brothers beating you and Jaspreet trying hard to stop them," I said.

"Oh... that would be tough, but as long as she is by my side, I'm ready to take on a few sticks," Gowtham expressed showing little fear.

"What if they kill you?" I giggled and Gowtham's expression changed.

"Who will kill whom, bhaiya? How are you?" a shrill voice suddenly greeted me. We turned to find Jaya standing behind us with her brown leather purse a little heavier than her in her right hand and a lady's pink colour handkerchief in the left hand.

"Hello! We were just kidding... I am good. This is my friend Gowtham," I introduced him and before I could ask her about Aridhita who was missing from the scene, we were greeted by another voice.

"Hello everyone! I guess you were talking about me or missing me. I am Aridhita Sharma."

She forwarded her right hand towards me, and paused for a second to shake hands. She had a strawberry flavoured softy in her left hand and her light pink lips had some ice cream on them which she licked with her light pink tongue in a flash when I pointed it out softly. She was wearing a pair of long earrings. She must have changed after office as she was dressed in casuals, unlike Jaya, who was in formals. She was pretty and had sharp features, greenish eyes, with a patch of her hair dyed golden. She was wearing a white kurta, dark blue denims and a light woolen jacket. She wasn't really hot, but definitely a smart girl who knew how to carry herself. She made her presence felt when she joined the conversation.

"No we were beginning to talk about you. You arrived right on time," I smiled as she gestured to all of us to move closer.

"How about having some burgers? I am really hungry," she said. We nodded and the burgers were ordered. The first half an hour of our meeting went discussing about how I had helped Jaya. I felt like James Bond who had helped a woman from drowning in an ocean. I was feeling embarrassed, not by the topic of discussion, but by Aridhita's constant gaze fixed on me. I wouldn't have noticed that until Gowtham messaged me.

Oh man! Why she is constantly staring at you? Clever chick!

Had he not messaged me, I would have been confident as I had been till that point. I got conscious, however, as I knew she was scrutinizing me.

"So what else do you do apart from helping girls on the road?" Aridhita asked me teasingly, tilting her head sideways with her eyes fixed on me.

"I am not a girl anymore," Jaya interrupted laughing.

Meanwhile, I tried gathering words which were clear a while ago but now scattered in my mind. I cleared my throat and without looking into her eyes, I described myself. Honestly, I was feeling timid. I had not felt that way for a long time. Yes, there had been some uncomfortable moments in the recent past due to my encounters with Eva, but not the nervous feeling that I was having. It took me an hour to get comfortable. Gowtham entertained us with his poor understanding of Hindi and his accent. Aridhita shared more about herself and I found her sweet after my initial assessment of her.

"....and then I told my manager, 'Sir, I am not going to stay in the office after seven. I am being paid for nine hours and I guess I am doing enough..." Aridhita laughed, describing her recent conversation with the manager.

"You should have seen my manager's face. By god he was as cute as Pokemon, but I had an upper edge and I left."

She laughed again. I was enjoying this. No matter how irritating a character is, girls find them cute. Her manager was short, bald, in his mid thirties and had been described like a pig earlier; even he ended up looking cute after the incident.

We all had a great evening. Meeting her face to face was a great experience. Gowtham was quite impressed by her. I guess he liked her, though I was sitting on the fence. Gowtham kept reminding me that it was to be a casual fling and would constantly bombard me with advice.

As Aridhita's office was close by, we would often plan to meet somewhere convenient. We would catch up for evening snacks. I enjoyed our brief meetings. She was very energetic and always on the move. She'd walk around the mall chatting about her future plans and her definition of a perfect guy, but would keep looking here and there as if she was expecting someone to come and greet her out of nowhere. She would look at me with such a sharp gaze that it would sometimes make me feel a little conscious. Her eyes seemed filled with feelings and emotions, compared to mine which were always steady and quiet.

"You are nice company," Aridhita said to me deep diving into my eyes. Her sentence gave me enough confidence and I was not uneasy.

"Even I like spending time with you," I reverted with a similar kind of look.

She untied her hair, letting her golden strands fall a little sideways, making her long face half visible. The dusk light falling on her made her more eye-catching. We were sitting on the top floor of Scope Minar which was at quite a height. We could see a beautiful bird's eye view of Delhi. We watched the city lights as dusk gradually turned into night time. It was slightly cold. Aridhita was just an inch away from me.

She was wearing a leather jacket, a dark green top, slightly showing the crystal triangular locket right in between her breasts. We were resting against each other with our shoulders.

"I so love to be with you," she said and rested her forehead on my shoulders. I was like a hero and felt on top of the world. I felt like a king with his queen beside him. I couldn't stay quiet when I kissed her forehead.

"Even I want to be…."

Thaap… thaap… thaap

I was disturbed by a loud thumping sound and realized that someone was patting my back roughly.

"Oh mister, can u wake up and check the mail?" a very harsh voice suddenly startled me.

"What the hell?" I said as I opened my eyes and turned around.

"Oh… Hi Teja sir. I am… sorry… I just…" I stammered. What else could I have said? I was caught red handed, sleeping in bright daylight just before lunch time. Gowtham stood next to Teja sir along with Chiya. Both of them were trying to control their laughter. I felt like a chicken who was helpless and about to get slaughtered. My mind was still on Aridhita as I looked around the office in a daze.

"Oh hero! The whole team is working hard. We are close to the delivery date and you are resting. What happened?" he taunted.

I tried to gather my thoughts. "Sir, I had a terrible night yesterday. I couldn't sleep because of a severe headache," I said squinting and trying to look sick.

Mr. Teja wasn't convinced and I couldn't think of anything else so asked him to verify with Gowtham who was my roommate. Teja sir looked at Gowtham without saying anything and that piercing look was more than enough to scare Gowtham who looked like he was going to piss in his pants.

"Aa...yes... he was unwell. Had a body ache and a stomach ache. I had to take him to the doctor," Gowtham stated getting confident and acting perfectly when there was no requirement. He didn't realize how idiotic he was seeming. He heard me telling the manager that I had a headache, so there was no need to mention any other ailment. Now who will handle Mr. Ghosh? Chiya looked at me in pity, but since she was about to burst into laughter, she left the scene. I was well awake now, forgetting what I had said in which mode. Gowtham had certainly screwed up everything.

"So you took him to the doctor? Nice!" Mr. Teja confirmed and Gowtham nodded.

"Since almost every part of your body seems to be aching, how are you managing chap?" he asked me innocently.

I couldn't make out whether he was taking my case or was genuinely concerned but I remained looking ill, recalling my days in Pune when Simer and I used to fool the trainers. The coordination between the two of us was remarkable and I was expecting something similar from Gowtham; he flunked miserably.

"Yes sir, I don't know how I am managing myself but I hope I will be fine..." I said in agreement. I saw no change in his expression, so I continued, "...and I will finish everything by tonight. I will work late."

"Ya fine..." he said and before turning around, he gave a scathing look at Gowtham. I was relaxed though, confident that I had convinced him. Before I could celebrate he stated sternly, "Do you guys think that I can be fooled at this level?"

"Pardon me!" I requested pretending that I had not heard him.

"I want the module to be ready by four. Start working on it rather than dreaming in daylight," he gave me an evil smile and continued.

"By the way, a very well formulated story. I will be watching the two of you from now onwards!" he taunted and left.

"Oh man! Why were you sleeping during office hours?" Gowtham asked teasing me, ignoring the fact that he would be under surveillance as well.

"Shut up! All because of you," I lashed at him.

"Oh, why me? Weren't you enjoying yourself dreaming about Aridhita?" he teased me.

For a second I wondered how he knew that I had been dreaming about her. Hope I wasn't talking in my sleep like him. That would be pretty embarrassing. But ignoring everything, I shouted again, "Yes, because of you. Please visit a doctor and get something for your sleeping disorders. I am tired of waking up when you snore or keep murmuring every night. I need a separate room."

"Aaahh... you are upset because of that! Don't worry, I have news for you, chose one out of the two fingers," he stated calmly, giving me two options in the form of his index finger and middle finger. Without further questioning, I quietly chose the index finger.

"Oh that's sad news, if you would have chosen the middle finger it would have been good news for you," he jumped in excitement pointing his middle finger at me. I picked up the register at my desk took a swipe at his finger.

"Can you please break the suspense?" I asked raising my eyebrows in rage.

"The bad news is that Rajshree has asked us to leave the room before the first of next month," Gowtham said abruptly with a smug face, knowing he had an important bit of information to share.

"What? Why?" I asked shocked.

"We are evicted because of your dealings with that haat chick Eva. Who asked you to go and hug her?" Gowtham said angrily as though he was really sad about being thrown out. I am sure he must be the happiest guy.

"I didn't do anything, and what's the good news?" I changed the topic.

"Oh yes… yes…" he said, paused and then continued.

"I have my uncle's flat in East of Kailash, near the Iskcon temple. We can shift and stay there…rent free," he said and winked at me.

"What the hell!" I said as his words sunk in. I paused for a moment and continued, "What did you say?" I asked with a smile.

"*Nee enna sevuda?* Can't hear me? Can't you get it in one go?"

"Shut up, Gowtham! Will you please tell me?"

"Okay man! Just teasing you…so we will shift next month after she throws us out," he said giving me a hi-five.

Gowtham was in love with Jaspreet. He was meeting her over cups of coffee, going for lunches together, and saving her from her manager's ire on many occasions. He often felt like a superhero and pictured a scene in the middle of a desert where a girl is being attacked by a group of anti-social people. Out of nowhere, a knight in shining armour appears, saves the girl and then lifts her, followed by a long ride that ends with a kiss. Such were his dreams which he narrated every moment he was with me or Chiya or at night when he talked in his sleep. He even gave me a contract; yes, a type of contract to write an email for her which he would deliver. Though it was a one-sided story, Gowtham was passionate and fiery. He handed me a pen drive and asked me to draft a letter as soon as possible so that he could woo Jaspreet.

I, on the other hand, received another mail from Contemporary Brat. The fact was that I hated the name, but each time the mail flashed in my inbox, it made me smile. I was happy that she had replied in a single line and that made me ping her immediately.

Hi Amateur,

You ping me on chat. I am available there.

Contemporary Brat.

Before I could think of pinging her, I received a call from Aridhita. A long 'hi' in her scintillating voice greeted me and I forgot what I was up to. She called and started describing her day, her manager, how funny her new reason was when he failed to stop her to work late hours. She was laughing whole heartedly, jumping in excitement and planning her future. I was listening attentively. She was fun to talk to and I was chuckling along with her. I had started wrapping up when she called, and was out of office in no time. She was going on merrily and suddenly asked, "By the way, where are you? I've just left office, so let's catch up near V3S Mall and..."she said this and before she could complete the sentence or I could gauge what she was going to say, I bumped into into someone while turning a corner.

"Wow! You are impossible. I can't believe it," she shouted at the top of her voice. It was Aridhita. I was in a state of shock. I was so lost in our conversation that I had not even realized that I had come five floors down, walked through the entire corridor, had come out of the gate and had walked in the direction of her office unknowingly. That was where I rammed into her. She thought that I had surprised her, but I was feeling embarrassed and worried about how I had left my desk. I had never even planned to meet her. I looked at her with a startled expression while she was beaming with excitement. I decided to laugh with her.

"Gosh! I never knew you'd be waiting for me. Are you like stalking me?" she grinned.

Though we were meeting almost every day, I always felt that it was a new beginning with her. She seemed different in each meeting. She would sometimes talk about her family, her cousins, would make fun of the manager; and sometimes she would seem restless while sitting at her favorite spot in the center of V3S mall, seem lost, looking here and there as though searching for someone.

I could see nothing wrong with her. She was pretty, smart, lively, and interactive. Perfect for a casual fling. That's what I was looking forward to anyway. I wondered how I'd proceed further. Should I tell her that I wanted a casual fling without any commitment? Should I start giving her hints about that temporary thing? But how can we define the criterion on the basis of which I can put a limitation on my feelings? Beyond a certain point, a line that divides love and time pass? How do people say that they are in a 'time pass' relationship? Do they sign a form or pre-decide? Or is it just the lust or attraction ruling over their minds against love or feelings that kill the inner consciousness? Whatever it was, I would be doing the same; getting into a fatal attraction, and living on the edge, hiding the love and just pure time pass.

I decided to ask her. I could see couples walking around holding hands, some fighting, some cuddling with each other, completely lost without paying any attention to the people around them. And then me and Aridhita separated by an inch of space. A gap still to be filled and a name to be assigned to what we will get into if I managed to say something. I decided to gather all the confidence after evaluating the pros and cons of what might be the end result. It could be a slap or a smile, it could be standing alone with all the people present in the mall staring at me and a few laughing when the girl leaves me, or it could be a hand in hand never-ending walk. I was prepared for both.

"Aridhita, will you…" I began when I was cut short and my words faded somewhere in her dominant question.

"Will you come with me? Come fast, let's go," she almost ordered and stood up. She turned towards me, stretched her hand to take mine and started running towards the elevator. How odd that was! It seemed as though we were being chased by someone.

"Where are we going? Why are we running?" I asked while getting into the lift. She pressed the second floor button and the elevator moved. I was looking at her, and she was gazing at me softly. That made me forget everything about what had happened in the last minute. Without wasting time, I began, "Aridhita, will you…." I started when the lift door opened and she dragged me out.

I was still trying to figure out what she was up to when she asked abruptly, "Will you hold my waist?" I was stunned but managed to stammer.

"Yes…aaa…no…what are you saying?" I questioned getting confused.

"Uff… you are just dumb. It's simple," she said getting irritated. She held my hand tightly and placed it on her waist gently as we walked towards the Spyker outlet. She was wearing a long sleeved blouse and navy blue slim fit trousers. She smiled at me and then asked me to hold her a little more tightly. With nervous hands but a confident look, I did that. She just drew herself closer to me and kissed my cheeks.

"Thank you, *sweetheart!* You are my *cutipie*," she stressed on the words 'sweetheart' and 'cutipie.' I noticed a guy staring at us as we crossed him. I was sure he had heard everything. I couldn't believe my luck. I never knew that without my saying anything, she had understood everything I had planned to say. Maybe that meant we seemed to be on the same page. I was living a dream, walking hand on waist with a beautiful girl in a mall, making everyone jealous. Her warmth was sufficient for me. We made two or three rounds holding hands like a couple. A few were staring, especially that one. I was enjoying myself. She was really fun to be with. Each time she crossed that guy, to tease him, she would kiss me. We crossed him a countless times. We named him the blue shirt guy as he was wearing a blue shirt with pitch black jeans.

We came out after spending an hour roaming in the mall. I had a wonderful time. She had her favourite strawberry ice-cream and now I was walking with her. She was looking beautiful. I was dreaming again: the thought of saying something that I planned an hour ago and getting a blushing yes which was obvious now, was exciting. We stopped for a moment at a place less crowded. The dim street light was perfect and I said, "Aridhita, will you be..." I began yet again only to be interrupted by her for the third time. It was getting a little frustrating.

"Shall I say something?" she stated without looking at me. I was thrilled, a little edgy and nodded confidently.

"I am really sorry for what I asked you to do inside. I was just behaving like a jealous bitch," she said, her face looking stern all of a sudden. She seemed guilty and she couldn't even look into my eyes.

"I didn't get you, Aridhita. I thought you were genuinely happy to be with me," I said with a faded smile. I wondered what she was up to and what was the reason for her sudden guilt.

"You are a sweet guy and I can't do this to you. I mean, I can't use you or just kill time by being with you," she looked at me and tears rolled down her cheeks.

Hold on! What did you just say? Use me or be with me just to kill time. Oh we were exactly on the same page. I am not a sweet guy, but a clever guy seeking a casual fling, but definitely not to hurt you. I just kissed a girl last week. Rather, she got the kiss out of me, but we kissed. I wanted to say all this to her, but she was crying. I just held her hand tightly and consoled her to make her feel better. She gently kissed me on my lips and we left. I guess things changed. I was sure that things could never be casual with her. In the end, one or the other would get hurt. I have to admit I was upset. I was feeling a little broken but I tried to be strong. The last peck on the lips was touching and I was truly moved.

"Oh man! You failed again," Gowtham laughed at me after I shared my misfortune with him. He laughed for at least fifteen minutes. He had tears in his eyes. *"Khushi ke aansu"*, he said. I was sitting with my hands folded and felt an urge to kick him hard.

"Do you think that's funny?" I asked him annoyed. Gowtham became quiet. He came close and sat down.

"Yes, I think it's very very funny," he sniggered and I kicked him. I maintained a few minutes' silence and then stated the exact reason for her behavior.

"I would have never let her go but the dilemma she was struggling with stunned me. She was another victim of a bruised ego. She was with me so that I could pacify her ego by being an object to be presented before someone who will be affected the most," I concluded with a sigh.

"But who will be affected the most by seeing her with you?" Gowtham asked perplexed.

"The guy in the blue shirt will be affected. The one who was staring at us," I said without looking at Gowtham.

"Stop kidding man! That guy was just a spectator who was jealous of you," he assured me. He thought that I was kidding.

"He was her ex-boyfriend Rakshyt or Rascal, who cheated on her. He promised to marry her, used her each time to have sex, to hang out and so on."

Gowtham remained silent and I continued.

"And she was trying to hurt his ego by proving to him that even she can have someone who can love her more than him. I was just a prop," I said quietly.

"Ohh that's mean of her," he said with an equally sad face.

"Either I get a girl who wants to kiss me because her boyfriend kissed her friend or slept with her, or I meet a girl who asks me to hold her from the waist and be all lovey dovey just to prove to her ex that she can get someone better than him," I expressed and before I could continue, Gowtham intervened.

threw a piece again but he didn't touch it. When I bit another one and threw the remaining half, he grabbed it.

"That's cool man! He is only eating your half, I can see two dogs eating the same biscuit," Gowtham jumped in excitement and giggled making fun of my achievement.

I don't know how but I did manage to convince him that we can befriend any dog; he also made an effort and fed the dog. His fear seemed to have evaporated as he fed another dog and tried chatting with them. I am sure he must be convincing them stating *maai tirupur, maai tamil, maai district maai biscuits..maai daags….*

The team was almost ready and was waiting for me to join so that they could start the training. The manager was ready with the manual to be dictated to us. The guys seemed to be over enthusiastic as all of them were newcomers. I felt like the odd one out who was still feeling the injustice of not being in Pune with Simer and the others. My current team was excited to be shifted to the client's side as conveyed by my new manager Mr Tej Ghosh. He was six feet tall with a fair complexion and thinning hair – proof of his experience and age. He was good in dictating things and his stern appearance made sure that one could not think of even sneezing. The black mole under his right eye reminded me of Teja in the movie *Andaaz Apna Apna* and the scene in which Paresh Rawal says '*Mark idhar hai, Teja main hu*'. The team was just nodding to what he was saying and he emphasised on moving to Laxmi Nagar, NIC customs office where we would be handling the project. As I listened to him, I reminded myself of my task of finding a girl. I started scanning my team once again; there were few girls, but honestly, most of them were failing the criteria, and before I could scan any further...

"Excuse me, Mister..." my manager asked, bringing me back to the session I was attending.

"Aren't you a part of the team and interested in shifting to the client location?" I said nothing but nodded like all the other ten heads around me. The manager ended with an enthusiastic speech, and the team winded up the session to break for lunch.

"Excuse me, you left your notebook," Chiya stopped me and before answering her I thought about my last meeting with her. She was the same girl who was sleeping while the manager was introducing me.

"*Tum thode gayab ho kya?* Are you feeling lost?" she asked me.

"No, not at all," I replied confidently, fearing her a little. She seemed to be our team leader. She said nothing and left the cabin with a smile that clearly indicated that she had found me stupid. While leaving she bumped into Gowtham who was walking lost in his thoughts.

"*Kahan dhyan hai? Dekhte nahi hum jarahe hain?* Pay attention to where you're going," she sneered at him and before he could say anything, she stormed off in a hurry.

"Stupid girl! It was clearly her fault. Bloody naarth Indians."

Gowtham saw me and pretended as if nothing had happened; but he noticed my silly grin and he couldn't resist yelling about her for the next ten minutes. I came to know from him that Chiya was from Lucknow, from a well-settled and deep-rooted cultured family of nawabs owning acres of land. Her father carried the legacy of the Singhs and held the major reins on the town they were settled in. She had inherited the habit of calling herself 'hum', an honored version of 'I'. In short, she was a confident girl who held that supremacy in her language and attitude. Yet she was grounded. Dusky complexion, healthy build with sharp eyes, she was lively and had a shrill voice; you could hear her even if you were sitting a kilometer away. She was in a long term relationship with a guy and the guy was as good as one could expect a guy to be. They were planning to get married within the next three months.

We shifted soon after the doctor gave us the green signal. It was just a single room with an attached bathroom, good enough for guys who are new to the corporate earning culture. The lady attendant named Raajshri was in service since the day she got married. Her two kids had almost completed their metric exams now. She showed us the room which she honestly confessed to have opened after three years and a chunk of garbage including decayed wooden furniture was moved out and cleaned. The sharp odor of the cockroach and mosquito repellant was enough to convince us that they have worked hard to convert the old maternity ward room into a guest room. It was a tough ask to stand in the room for even a second. The walls were patchy and the cupboard doors had been left open to ventilate the insides. The ceiling fan was well polished but the switch near the door was half broken. Gowtham took his handkerchief out and started sneezing; the lady looked at him sideways and said, "You can shift elsewhere if you have a problem with the room." She spoke as if she had been given full authority to cancel the deal finalized by the owner herself.

Before Gowtham could say anything offending to the lady in charge, I intervened.

"It's perfect; where else could we find such a refreshing place and that too at decent rate."

I pinched Gowtham and pacified him.

"The only *guuud* thing about Delhi is that we will for eternity never be short of beauties around us," Gowtham stated staring at the girl in shorts, who moved in to the metro station with us, definitely ignoring us as if she knew that she had given us a topic to discuss at the Mayur Vihar metro station. We got our smart cards issued, and before we could take the escalator, Gowtham frowned.

"Aah.. *kodomay* mismatch!"

"What mismatch?" I asked puzzled.

"*Kodomay...ko-do-may* means *haarible*. Why do I have to state clearly what you can notice clearly?" He shouted at me.

"Oh horrible," I thought and decided not to correct his pronunciation.

"...And the worst part about Delhi is that all the beauties will be with a security guard and that guard will be her *baayfriend*," he wailed as I saw the same girl in white shorts hugging her guard, I mean her boyfriend. He felt further mortified and I could see where the word *kodomay* appplied. The girl was cute, while the less said of her boyfriend the better.

"I love my Tirupur; good culture and no hugging and showing of emotions at my place. Girls look better in dresses..." he could see them following us on the next elevator towards the platforms.

"Ya man, relax. Why are you getting pissed off? It's simply called the law of role reversal."

"What's that? Could you please elaaborate?" Gowtham asked.

Meanwhile we had boarded the train and the couple who had offended Gowtham also got in with us. I could see the guy holding her left hand, resting on the opposite door, and girl standing holding the support. We both positioned ourselves in the middle just at the centre of two opposite doors. I could see Gowtham still trying to gape at the girl, but as he turned towards the skinny figure holding her hand, he would grimace.

"The law of role reversal is nothing but a feeling of pleasure by placing yourself in someone else's boots the moment you feel offended," I said staring out through the running metro which had just started.

"If you would have been with that girl, then any other guy watching you would have felt the same way. You'd be just a guard or a gardener for them." I giggled.

It was Saturday evening and as I looked around, the couples around me seemed restless. They were all on their way to hang out, date and have fun. Those in relationships seemed lost in the warmth of the metro while amateur couples seemed self conscious and coy. Young people in groups were busy discussing all the events at tuition centers, colleges, and schools. The middle-aged crowd was silent. Some had ear phones plugged in their ears thinking and imagining a better version of life with the rhythm of the song they were playing, while a few were staring at the youth blankly, smiling and trying to imagine what they were like at this age. Those who were left were like us, either finding faults in the couples or searching for wandering souls like ourselves, but definitely in the opposite sex.

"I didn't understand anything about that law of reversal, but I am sure this girl is not happy with this guy," Gowtham said swinging in between the passage.

"How can you say that I asked dividing my looks between Gowtham and the couple.

"I think the girl wants to be with me. I noticed her expression clearly stating that she committed a mistake by saying yes to this guy," Gowtham affirmed persistently staring at the girl, forgetting that she was with someone. I could see her holding hands and trying to get cozy with her boy playing with her phone. I guess her glance at Gowtham had made him confident about her. That proved that how positive he could be even after receiving a defiant look from the girl.

I have been to Delhi many times. My uncle used to stay in Delhi way back when I was a school going boy. I was never fascinated by Delhi; you will often find people saying that Delhi is fast, things move fast, people are smart, little brash, unproductive and flashy. I was wondering how fast life can be when I noticed the guy changing his expression to a sardonic look and holding the girl's hand tightly. For a second I thought he would hug her or do something cheesy, but the firmness in the hold suggested possessiveness with the hint of a little aggression. He said something that made that cute girl try to snatch her phone from him. The boy remained unmoved. Gowtham and I shared a look. What was going on? A part of the crowd shifted their eyes on them.

'Next station is Noida sector -18. Doors will open on the right.'

The announcement was bang on time and people prepared to disembark. We were also being pushed with the flow but I was little curious to know what would happen next. We however lost the sight of the couple. We flashed our smart cards at the exit and moved out from the gate closer to the GIP mall. Before we could take the stairs, I could see the couple near the exit stairs. They seemed to be settling things that had gone out of control a while ago.

"How can you cheat on me? He has written that he is missing you? Can you explain that?" he said as he wiped the sweat off his face in despair. Before we could hear the girl's explanation, I pushed Gowtham and we moved on.

"Where are you lost, Gowtham? We are getting late."

We moved ahead and turning my head back could only notice the girl trying to pacify him with a little disgusted look. Maybe she was feeling conscious about a scene being created. The sound of conversation washed out and running crowd discolored my view of checking on what happened next. I know that it was stupid of us peeping into other people's lives, but that was something Gowtham had never witnessed before. I have seen couples fighting, and many times I had been questioned when I was in a relationship, but for Gowtham it was something new. And never in front of a crowd at the metro station. I was thinking about how the journey between the few stations changed the relationship. Had they been fighting fifteen minutes back, Gowtham would have confirmed that the girl was fighting with the guy because she had fallen in love with him.

It was time to pay attention to my 'leisure hunt'. If I leave Gowtham, even I was stuck on an underprivileged thought of discovering someone I could date, as per the notion of 'Leisure hunt' given by Shikha. But honestly, what kind of bizarre search was it. We all are moving in life with such a thought. Who wants to be single when you know you have ample time to find and date someone. So it was on, but finding someone by walking on the streets, or roaming in a mall, or booking tickets or hanging in the metro to keep an eye on girls who were travelling with their so called baadyguards was all nonsense. But with Gowtham, the search was fun. Gowtham was being positive about everyone around him, imagining a perfect match for me and himself.

"*Intha ponnugale ippadi thanda,*" Gowtham said confidently. He looked at me and translated.

"All girls are the same…bus, train *madhiri onu poonaa innonnu varum*, so no worries."

He went on rambling, but I couldn't get anything. I was left with a big question mark with not so soothing expressions when he translated.

"I mean to say that they are like a bus, or a train. One will go, another will come, so no worries man!" he exclaimed.

"Oh, even you south Indians have the same thought. Wow!" I said amused and giggled.

"Ya man! It's universal law, but it's naat saaouth Indians. That's my Tamil, my Tirupurr, my lovely district. Do you mind?"

He expressed loudly, catching the attention of the people close by.

And It Happened...

"I will kill you, Agent Smith...Agent Smith, you can't kill Rajni."

"I will kill you, Agent Smith...Agent Smith, you can't kill Rajni."

"Who is this fucking Agent Smith?"

I woke up half asleep trying to gain consciousness. Rubbing my eyes, I tried to locate my cell phone. It was three o'clock. I turned my head towards Gowtham to find him staring at me. Gosh! He scared me.

"Are you awake?" I asked him getting a little nervous, but he got up at once and asked.

"Where is Smith?"

He was being really weird. He didn't seem to recognize me and called me Morpheous, and he called himself Agent Neo. I suddenly recalled what my teammates had told me about his witch attacks. But I guess he had a sleeping disorder called Somniloquy; in simpler words, he was sleep-talking. I guess he was in Matrix mode, but where did Rajni figure in that. He might have mixed tamil movie and matrix together. I pointed in the other direction and he followed my finger, only to turn towards his bed, close his eyes and doze off.

There was a knock on the door. I opened my eyes when I found the knock a little harder and irritating. It was 9.00 a.m.

on Sunday. I searched for my slippers and opened the door to find Raajshri, the same woman who had shown us the room, standing there.

"Someone wanted to see you," she said giving me an impish smile. Rubbing my half-open eyes, I heard another voice.

"Hi, I am Eva. Aunty told me that two guys were staying on the third floor, so I thought I must meet them. We should know who our neighbors are, right?"

My blurred vision cleared and zoomed in on the figure standing next to Raajshri aunty. I shook my head to check what I was seeing was for real. It was clear. I could see a figure wearing peach coloured shorts with long waxed legs, a deep necked light grey top ending just above a pierced belly button and a body as clean and smooth as one after a shower and body lotion. The chilly morning with no sun had no effect on the girl who was covering herself with a cardigan long enough, finishing above her knees. Her wet hair and shining drops of fresh bath water were merging perfectly with the foggy weather outside. She was holding an armful of clothes which I guess were put to dry in the verandah last night. She was standing and leaning on her left leg. I could see all sorts of variety that were latest in fashion or trendy wrinkled, strangled and left half dead in her right hand. But I was awake now, as conscious as if put on an ATM duty. I confidently introduced myself and told her about Gowtham who was snoring loudly. He sounded like a howling wolf. Eva and aunty couldn't resist giggling.

"Ya, it was good you took the initiative. At least we can all turn to each other if anything is ever needed," I replied as genuinely as one could be.

She told me about her roommate Medha who worked even on Saturdays, and if required, on Sundays as well. Eva was from Agra. She had completed her MBA in HR from a not so recognized institute. Her face frowned on asking about the university. But if you observe, that's what we are all doing: studying what the herd is, getting admissions in numerous self-acclaimed number one institutes and then hardly respecting the university and being ashamed of naming it, admitted Eva with a straight sad face. My eyes tried not to look down below her chin or her glossy body. While chatting, she dropped one of the clothes she was holding. Before I could react to it and assist her, she bent down quickly, revealing more than what one could desire. Her deep neck top was loose enough to show a cream-coloured strapped new fashioned bra. The perfect shapes that I witnessed unwillingly resulted in my eyes going wide opened and made me feel like releasing heat through my ears.

Shifting my eyes somewhere else and pretending to have witnessed nothing, I just smiled when she said, "These bras are as slick as my relation with my guy," she stated something out of context but it was her capricious thought in a flow. Maybe she was conscious that I saw her private fabric or maybe she was just too talkative and blunt to hide even a pinch of emotion. I was startled by her offhand candour. I pretended to take no notice and instead turned around to check if Gowtham was up. I just smiled as I turned to her again.

"It was cool meeting you, buddy. See ya soon," she chirped and shook my hand before leaving. I stayed reliving the moment. How electrifying it was! I had already started thinking about her. How quick I was. She was nothing like Priety or Riya... the former my lost love and the latter whom I lost before realizing it was love. I was done looking for my lost love in every girl. Eva might turn out to be my hot girlfriend. Wow!

Laxmi Nagar - V3s Mall

The team of ten shifted to Scope Minar near V3s Mall, Laxmi Nagar. We were all relieved as we found this new location closer and more suitable, as it was in the city itself. We could see a healthy crowd around unlike the out-of-the-way, deserted Greater Noida. The only drawback of the new place was the office which was like a typical civil hospital building: the elevators were as old as the Delhi fort walls, painted and designed with regular pan splatter by government officials who were feeling pleased after handing over their chunk of work to us. They were our respective clients, and whatever they did and demanded, we had to oblige. Those were the instructions engraved in our MNC's nomenclature.

"Oh no! *Kodomay* washrooms," Gowtham expressed his grief while entering the loo. He was right. Atrocious it was and stinking like hell. The sinks were jammed and poor drainage systems made sure that the floor of the washroom was always wet. This was the state of all government office restrooms perhaps.

"Enaku kastakalam da unkuda," Gowtham said something in Tamil.

"What do you mean?" I asked with a weird face.

"I am having worst time since the time I have met you." Gowtham hollered at me. I gave him a startled look and he explained.

"I got a stinking room with you at that poor maternity ward, then this government hospital of an office and now these filthy washrooms," he pointed looking at me through his grey frames, his eyes wider than normal and eyebrows raised, while we were fixed against the wall releasing ourselves in the washroom. I paid little attention to his remarks, knowing his nature of shouting and blabbering at anything without any reason. I kept a straight face.

It's easy to change his line of thought so I asked him, "Which films did you watch during this weekend?" I zipped my jeans to move towards the pan splattered washbasin.

"What does that have to do with the tough time I am having with you?" he asked finishing his quota and joining me at basin and staring me through the mirror.

"Did you find Agent Smith who tried to kill Rajni sir, you poor Mr Neo?" I asked rinsing my hands.

"I did watch Matrix and my favorite Rajini movies, but how come you are asking me about the characters?" Gowtham asked with his mouth open.

"I am being deprived of sleep since the time I have been with you because of you being a fucking agent and your constant rattling because of your sleep disorder. Did I complain about that?" I asked pretending to be serious when I noticed his puppy face with an expression as if found guilty of something. I turned towards the exit and he followed me quietly.

"Please zip up your pants, what you're wearing inside might become the talk of the day," I giggled and he reacted instantly only to find his pants already zipped.

"Bloody *dyaam* you are…rascala…" he screeched and I loped away.

It was a frosty evening and I was sitting on the terrace. I had no option as my room was on the terrace. I was well insulated in my black sweat shirt. It was the kind of weather where one should be in a room with the heater on and a packet of groundnuts to munch on. I was feeling bored and thought of getting my guitar and giving it a try. I had had it with me since my college days and had not gone beyond a couple of leads.

I had hardly played anything when I noticed someone repeatedly calling my name rather urgently. I could see it was Gowtham who had come running up to the third floor, exhausted, impatient to convey something that he had just discovered.

"I have great news for us!"

"What's that?" I tried to concentrate on playing my guitar. He immediately reacted. He snatched the guitar, grabbed a chair and sat on it.

"Man! You won't believe this, I just saw a bombshell and a cute girl on the second floor. I guess the girls have moved in and now we can find one..."

Before he could complete his sentence we were greeted by another soft voice.

"Hey! Hi!"

It was Eva. She came and greeted me, shook hands and smiled as if we were good friends.

"How was your day? How have you been? What are you doing here? I guess you must be having office ha, cool weather you know."

One statement and too many questions, and most self-answered.

I was just standing observing her; she was restless and didn't notice that Gowtham was staring at her with his mouth open. I smiled as she blabbered. Gowtham unknowingly ran his fingers on the guitar strings, only to produce an unpleasant sound that stopped her from jabbering and allowed me to introduce Gowtham to her.

She greeted him nicely, shook hands and left him awestruck. He held her hand firmly and she pulled it out giving him a weird look.

"It's nice that you play the guitar," she addressed Gowtham with a smile, complementing him. She insisted him to play a track and how could he say no when he was holding the guitar like a *sitar*.

"Thank you...but I play Tamil saangs, you will hardly understand that, so let him play a nice saang for you."

Pointing towards me, he handed me the guitar and left me in a situation where I could not say no to the bombshell who cutely added a long pleeeasseee.

Now what do you expect? In a movie, the guy out of the blue, with no knowledge of an instrument and pathetic vocals will suddenly start to sing the song of his life with the perfect lyrics. Snow will begin to fall and the girl will look like a fairy while the neighbours will join the chorus. Finally the guy with the shy smile on his face will win the heart of the woman. Bullshit!

I tried playing a few leads of Bollywood tracks which she could recognize. I fumbled with the rhythm but Gowtham seemed impressed because he hardly understood anything.

"I am just an amateur," I justified and my introvert gesture got a big thank you out of her and she half hugged me.

"I wish my boyfriend could play something for me," she said and complemented me as if I had discovered the rhythm she had lost somewhere. I was enjoying this; she was good but now she was even better. Gowtham started signaling at me and gave me an impish smile. I glared at him. I was wondering if I was too dumb or was she someone who liked little things? But I found her sweett. The guy problem! I told you I guess.

"Dumb!" she exclaimed, suddenly changing her expression from cheerful to remorseful. Did she reply to what I was thinking a second ago? Was I really dumb?

"My boyfriend is dumb, he doesn't even care," she stated and I felt relieved. It was addressed to someone else. I guess it was the third time she tried involving her boyfriend in our conversation and I couldn't resist asking about him. I guess it was a mistake.

It was a story that started at 10.00 p.m. Let me remind you it was a cold winter night, and we were on the terrace. It ended almost after half past eleven. Gowtham quit the gathering about forty-five minutes before the end when he received a call from his hometown. All the while I sat numb in the cold with my hands in my pockets. I was trying hard to not shiver in front of someone who apparently thought I was her best buddy! It seemed this beauty with no brain would make me skip dinner as well.

"I think we will break up soon; I am done with him. He is getting on my nerves. He was never like this. He is trying to curb my freedom," she lamented and expected me to say something. Meanwhile Gowtham joined us again. I would have advised her like any other guy, but due to the biting cold, I decided to give her genuine advice, though she was one of the options I was considering for myself.

"You should talk to him; the method you shared with me will work well if you share your thoughts with him. There is no point keeping things inside yourself and ending your relationship before hearing what he has to say," I said like a perfect teacher and noticed her paying attention. In between I noticed Gowtham trying hard to signal something. I guess he did not like my suggestion. Ignoring him, I continued.

about her when she didn't even bother to show up! I got a little agitated and reacted.

"Even I hate that name! It sounds illogical, brash, stupid and nonsensical and...." I ran short of words when she interrupted.

"...and weird," she completed my sentence and we both laughed. We chatted for some time while walking into the temple complex. We climbed the stairs and she started describing the temple and how many times she has visited the place as she adored Lord Krishna. She told me how bored she was at her uncle's place. She had then decided to visit the temple and found me. Some company was better than no company. I had almost forgotten about Contemporary Brat when I received another text from her while I was taking off my shoes at the shoe counter.

Mr Amateur,

I thought of giving you a surprise but all guys are the same. Huh! I saw you with another girl. Goodbye forever.

Never yours

Contemporary Brat

How was I to know that she had planned a surprise for me? I was getting edgy; it was like somebody was playing games and I was in no mood to participate. It was really frustrating. I decided to call her right away. I was about to dial her number when Shikha came.

"Did you get the token? *Chalo fir,* lets attend the *aarti.* It's really beautiful upstairs. Come fast!" she ordered and I had to follow her as she ran quickly, before I could even ask her to excuse me for a second. I tried her number nevertheless but it was switched off. Damn!

We entered the hall which was lit up with bright lights. The hall was golden hued. Chanting in the name of Lord Krishna was going on in full swing. Some people were dancing while others were lost in his prayers. Some were even crying as they stared at the idol. I was wondering how can one cry staring at the idol; it was like everyone was under marijuana effect. A young fleet of pandits dressed in white kurtas and dhotis with red tilaks on their foreheads were *magna* dancing. A few ladies were singing in chorus and going round in a circle chanting the Lord's name. The atmosphere was so electrifying that even an atheist would start believing in Krishna's power. Such was the aura inside the temple. We were just in time for the darshan aarti. It was awesome to see the rituals. I was engrossed in the scene when I saw the figure standing next to me, lost in a different world. Her eyes were closed. She was murmuring continuously. I could see her lips moving apart and heard her chanting *'Hare Krishna hare Rama'*. As I watched Shikha, it seemed as though just the two of us existed at that moment. I could not hear anything; I was just watching her. She couldn't be any prettier. I gave a quiet thanks to Contemporary Brat for not showing up. I would have missed a good time with Shikha. As the fifteen-minute aarti ended, Shikha completed her prayers, her folded hands then touching them at her forehead and then sliding through the nose, kissing them, and before I could notice she opened her eyes and caught me staring at her.

"What?" she questioned me, raising her right eyebrow. I said nothing and instead pretended to be engrossed in ending my prayers. We collected our shoes and then came out of the temple. We stood at the place where we had met. It was close to eight when Shikha said, "I think I should leave now, it's really late," she said without looking at me.

"Yes, it is quite late," I said with a smile but I was looking at her. She nodded and before she could say anything, I sneaked my hand into my pocket and took the light pink flower out of it. Some of the petals were crushed but the flower was still holding its grace even after three hours in my pocket. I had got it for Contemporary Brat. I decided to give it to Shikha.

"Aah… wow! When did you get this? Is it for me?" she questioned in excitement. She accepted it gracefully and thanked me.

She suddenly stared at me long and hard and said, "I never knew you were going to meet me here. Thank you for the wonderful time, Mr Amateur," she said. We shook hands, smiled and parted. I started walking towards my flat feeling a little sad. One, I had not met Contemporary Brat, and Shikha also left.

I was feeling a little low and was still lost as I recalled Shikha's last expressions, the way she had smiled and waved me goodbye. I remembered her last sentence and how sweet she sounded when she had said '*Thank you for the wonderful time, Mr Amateur*'. Just wow! Just… just a moment, what did she say? Mr Amateur! Is it? I was stunned. I stopped walking and immediately turned back to see if she was still there. But she was gone. I was taken aback.

Shikha was Contemporary Brat!

It had all been planned. It took a while for everything to sink in. I was trapped again but this was something funnier. I could recall our chats when she used to say '*You are learning quick*', her abrupt statements like check the meaning of '*cum*' and similarly when she met me in the train and said that '*if guys can have fun, so can I, even I am going through multiple affairs, arre buddhu, just kidding*'…I could recall the way she had tried fooling me in the train. It was all planned, and she was quite smart. She messaged me at the right time when I was getting a token at the shoe counter and didn't allow me to call. She is the one with whom I was chatting. She knew me, and the only coincidence was that we started blogging on the same website. The girl who introduced the thought of '*When Love Meets Ego*' had been in constant touch with me. She was not only reading but directing my blogs as well. The more I thought about it, the more excited I got. I was sure I'd meet her again. I took my phone and before I could dial her number, I received a call.

'Contemporary Brat calling.'

I picked her call and she laughed for a few minutes. I didn't mind, though I wondered what she was laughing about.

"Arre buddhu, turn around."

She disconnected the call and I turned back when she almost half hugged me. I was feeling awesome but it was my puppy face that drew more attention.

As we walked back towards my flat, she kept on telling me how she had made a fool out of me, how she enjoyed reading my blogs though she didn't like most of them, and how happy she had been when I mailed her for the first time. I opened the door and we entered my new flat. She came and sat in my room. I was looking at her when she became quiet and said, "Don't think of ever misbehaving with me."

We both laughed. She was a little conscious when she saw me pulling the guitar out from the bag. I sat down on the bean bag right in front of her.

"Will you play for me?" she asked.

I nodded with a smile, adjusting my guitar to fine tune it. I asked her to open the drawer and take out a pick for me. She turned to the study table. She opened the drawer to find a red rose inside it. She paused for a moment. She was about to turn towards me, but she didn't. She seemed hesitant to pick it up, but when she did, she found a light pink envelope addressed to 'Dear Contemporary Brat'. She picked the card and turned towards me. Before she could say anything I gestured to her to keep quiet with my fingers on my lips and asked her to focus on my song.

I started with an instrumental and then I tried to sing for her. A song from the movie *What's your Rashee?*

Tum jo ho to gaa rahi hai yeh hawa,
Tum jo ho to reshami si hai fiza,
Jao na jao na jao na….

Hoo phir naa yeh raat aayegi,
Phir naa yeh rutt chhaegi,
Phir naa yu milna hoga,
Phir naa jaane kya hoga?
Jao na jao na jao na….. haan…

I tried ending with the final leads because I could play only that much of the song. It was tough playing guitar and I was faltering. I hope she had not noticed. I glanced at her and she seemed quite overwhelmed by my performance. She was vibrant before I played, but she was silent then, her expressions were soothing, her eyes were a little dense, her vibes were receptive and her voice went low.

"Is it for real?" she finally asked without blinking her eyes, and looking intensely at me.

I nodded with a smile. I gestured to her again to open the second drawer and she did. There was something wrapped in gift paper with rose petals strewn all over it. She lifted it up and looked at me. Before opening it, she asked me to come close to her. She was sitting on the revolving chair next to the study table holding the gift. She seemed a little nervous. She was staring softly at me. She gestured to me to sit down and I knelt down to sit opposite her.

"Is this for me?"

I nodded again and smiled at her. She was looking gorgeous.

"Why? Why are you doing this?" she whispered. I looked at her and smiled again.

"You surprised me in a way I could never have imagined, so it's my turn now."

"Can you open it for me?" she asked holding out the gift. I untied the yellow ribbon and the light orange gift wrapper with golden lining. I was checking her expression. She seemed happy. I pulled out the little basket which had a cute teddy bear sitting at the center and had chocolates around it covered with petals. There was a card in it which she picked up and it read:

Contemporary Brat,

The gift will be special if the eyes that are meant to see it pass on the message to her lips that will end up with a smile which will last forever.

With luv,
Amateur

She read it and a smile lit up her face. It was a different smile; it had a spark in it. I was so lost in watching her sitting a few centimeters away when she bended forward towards me. Her left hand held my head, and in a flash, her lips rubbed against mine. This was one long kiss which I owned. Her eyes were closed; I glanced at her eyelids and the right one had a light brown mole on it. She opened her eyes and released me, but kept me just an inch away and whispered, "You hate my name. Contemporary Brat. Weird, stupid, illogical and ..."

"...and awesome...aa... lovely and thoughtful. I love it..." I completed and she kissed me again passionately. As I compared to what had happened in the past with Eva and Aridhita, I realized that their kisses were to satisfy their egos, but the kiss with Shikha was marked with my name and it had the intensity to prove that it was out of genuine feelings and nothing else. But a kiss on our first meeting was something I had never expected.

The MBA Class

The office days were passing better; the separate rooms in the new flat gave me the much needed relief. However, I couldn't sleep at all. I'd meet up with Shikha at Laxmi Nagar before coming home. I would then talk to her as I had dinner followed by a chat before midnight and one after. If I happened to be sleepy after a long day's work, she'd say, "You hardly give me any time. Stay busy huh," she would complain before disconnecting the call. She however would pick up at the first ring when I'd call back.

"Why do you have to disconnect the call when I was just kidding?" I would say stifling my yawn.

"Oh my sweet liar, I am feeling scared, so talk to me. My roommate has gone," she would say in such a tone that I would be ready to face any ghost she was scared of.

"Don't worry, I am here," I would say something like that as if I was Salman Khan ready to protect her. So went our conversations at night. Cozy and drowsy under the quilt, muttering sweet nothings.

Shikha shared a flat with two other girls in Laxmi Nagar. She'd meet me daily after work and then would study on her own at home. The rest of the time she'd spend talking to me on the phone. It had become a fixed routine.

It was Friday when I was supposed to meet her at Rajiv Chowk. She had forced me to take leave as she wanted to take me along for the registration of the coaching classes for MBA. I took the metro from Pragati Maidan where she was waiting for me and got down with her at Rajiv Chowk. It was a long walk to the coaching centre from the metro station.

We entered the centre. Shikha was excited to join the classes and kept on telling me how she was desperate to study further after being the university topper. She had wasted a year listening to a guy who would not allow her to study because he never wanted her to be independent and work.

As I listened to her past, I thought of Eva and Aridhita. I couldn't resist asking her about him and wondered if he was still a part of his life.

"When did you leave him?" I asked her.

"He was the same guy I told you about while we were coming back from Bandra to New Delhi, hope you remember?" she said. I recollected our conversation but then I questioned her that if he was the guy who had just proposed to her then, how had she wasted a year?

"Ma'am, here is your card and you can collect the study material from that counter," the lady at the reception instructed her. She walked towards the counter and I followed.

"No...I lied to you. We were in a relationship for three years. Nothing wrong with him; he loved me and I loved him. Then one fine day he cheated on me. It was my birthday. Everybody in my family knew about us and it was tough. I was so into him that I had given up my space. I always thought that he was caring, but he was curbing my freedom. Right from keeping tabs on my phone to reading all my messages to calls every moment we were apart. He then declared that the relationship was over. I thought this was love. When someone is so into you each and every moment, then how could he cheat on you? When I was there body and soul for him," she stated and I could see her eyes filling up, a hint of regret and pinch of tear covering the enigmatic eyes she was wearing *kajal* in. I could feel her pain and I was sad, a little jealous as well.

"Here are your books and material. Good luck for your classes," the man at the counter handed her the material which I volunteered to carry for her. She signed the register and thanked him. She remained quiet and I began thinking.

It was another case of failed love. Wasn't it the case everywhere? No, it wasn't! Not every relationship is bad. I thought about Chiya and her boyfriend. They were meant for each other and had been together for eight years. They were to get married soon. Love exists and relationships do have a value, but what about those souls who feel broken after facing the betrayal from someone they had shared their space with? The sense of insecurity and hatred shattering the dreams of two people being together. I was trying hard to not think about Shikha, but I couldn't resist the thought of making her life better; giving her love and treating her right was dominating my mind.

"I still miss him and I feel if I could be with him..." she expressed and I cut her short.

"So you must ask him, forgive him and get back to him," I suggested.

"Once a cheat is always a cheat. I can't go back to him. And who are you to give me advice?" she said and I was hurt by her remark. She noticed my glum expression and changed the topic smartly.

"Why are you sad, my lover boy? Of course I respect your advice, but now I have moved on," she said and I was touched by the words 'lover boy'. Priety used to call me by this name and it was a pure twist of fate. The past was the past, that was true. You move on and you move on to something better.

It had become my routine to pick her from her coaching classes, and spend some time with her. We'd go on a stroll, sometimes watch a movie, and then during weekends, she would love to visit the Iskcon temple. She'd stay back at my place and would leave on Sunday.

It was one of those Saturdays when she called me before her class began.

"Why do you want me to come at nine? I guess the class gets over by two."

"I don't know, just tell me whether you are coming or not?"

What else could I say when she asked me like that. I reached well in time and waited outside the building when I saw her running towards me. She was looking different. She was wearing a printed casual sleeveless top with light blue fitted denims. Gosh! She really carried herself well. All I wanted to do was kiss her. It was tough controlling myself as I looked at her lips while she spoke to me. Her roving eyes made me look deep into them. Her shaking head made me notice the pretty earrings she was wearing, her falling hair on one side and the light grey frames of her spectacles. I could see her shining arms as she waved them while speaking to me. I was getting more attracted towards her with each passing moment. I was lost when she stamped her foot on mine.

"What are you thinking?"

"Aah... nothing... just wanted to know where we are going. I don't think you will ask me to wait till one," I said.

"Aww! Do you think that I am that rude to keep my baby waiting?" she said teasing me and touching my right cheek. She had used the word 'baby' for the first time, and honestly, I liked it.

"We are not going anywhere; you will attend the class with me," she said. That was a surprise! As she started walking towards the building, I wondered how'd I attend the class. I didn't have a notebook with me. For god's sake I didn't even have my name registered. I ran after her.

"Are you kidding? I am not even registered here; they will kick me out," I said annoyed.

"Calm down and just follow me" she said with authority as if she had my name registered. She walked straight towards the parking lot rather than turning right towards the stairs to the first floor. I followed her. As we entered the parking lot, it was a little dark. She took a right, walked a few steps and then turned left to find an empty spot hidden from normal vision. Before I could ask her anything, she pulled me towards herself and put her fingers on my lips.

"Shhhh... I found this spot yesterday," she whispered pulling me closer. I loved it but I was a little nervous about getting caught by a guard or someone parking his or her vehicle. I looked around anxiously but gained confidence when I realized the spot was rather well hidden. She opened her purse, and took out something.

"Which one would you prefer to taste?" she held two lip glosses – one was strawberry flavoured and the other had the flavor of a fruit smoothie. I chose strawberry and smiled at her.

"Okay fine! Now close your eye," she winked at me and said. I followed without questioning.

"How desperate are you!" she taunted me to get a raised eyebrow look from me. What did I do? I am just following your instructions, I said in my mind. She applied it on her lips and stared deep into my eyes which I couldn't close. Giving a mischievous smile, she put her arms around my neck and lifted her feet to stand on her toes. I automatically wrapped my arms around her waist to hold her tightly.

She whispered, "I wanted to kiss you here yesterday and I..."

Before she could complete her sentence, I couldn't resist and sealed her lips. I felt the strawberry flavour while rubbing them softly and we were lost in the moment. She held my hand softly and placed it above her waist. I could feel her bosom pressed against my chest. The feel was strong, the moment was seductive. She hugged me tightly.

"Do you want to try the fruit smoothie flavor?" she teased me with a spark in her eyes. They were illuminated and I was drowning in them. I nodded and she punched me hard and ran away shouting, "Mr Amateur, who do you think will attend the class then?" her voice echoed and I ran after her.

I got an entry into her class. Trust me, my legs were shaking and my heart beat faster out of fear. I could feel the difference: between one because of the kissing and other because I was committing fraud. I never knew Shikha had already stolen an ID card, and had replaced someone's ID photo with mine. My new name was Farhaan. I was afraid I wouldn't be able to pull it off. Shikha asked me to say that I had missed my classes in the previous batch so I had joined this batch. She was smart as she picked the right card. Most of the time I hid my face by covering it with both my palms and not at all looking at the lecturer. We sat on the very last bench. She found it thrilling and adventurous, but I was nervous. I was pretending to be a sincere student with an attentive face. Shikha was mischievous. She took my notebook and started making two hearts meeting each other. She began a game of zero-cross with me, and moved on to jumbled words using censored and seductive words. Suddenly she wrote:

Do you want to taste the fruit smoothie flavour?

I looked up at her in surprise.

"Here? Right now? Are you crazy?" I whispered. She nodded.

I nodded as well and she pulled the lip gloss out. I made a face at her which was unfortunately noticed by the lecturer who interrupted my titillating thoughts of kissing Shikha sitting on the back bench.

"Hello Mister? Can you please answer this?'

I stood up as he asked me the solution to the problem which was clearly written on the white board. With a body half-paralyzed due to anxiety, I tried reading the problem.

Find the odd man out. 445, 415, 109, 53, 25,11,4?

Was it a coincidence? Or had the professor caught me? I couldn't think when I read the words 'odd man out'. I was the odd one out sitting there and was planning to kiss a student of the class. The professor repeated the question. I could see that most of the people around me were concentrating hard on solving the problem.

Without taking much time, I said, "It's 415," ready to be told by the professor that I was wrong. I looked disappointed and was about to sit down when he said, "Yes, it's correct."

I smiled with pride, but that only lasted till he questioned me again.

"How did you derive this conclusion?"

I became numb. Before I could think of anything, Shikha kicked me and silently slid her notebook towards me, which already had the answer. I was confident again as if someone had injected a life drug into my body. I read it out loud:

"Sir, to obtain the next number, we have to subtract 3 from the previous number and divide the result by 2
445
(445-3)/2 = 221
(221-3)/2 = 109
(109-3)/2 = 53
(53-3)/2 = 25
(25-3)/2 = 11
(11-3)/2 = 4

That is how 415 is the odd number. You can taste the fruit smoothie after class."

"Come again? What did you say? Fruit smoothie?" The Professor enquired as if he had heard wrong. I pretended to be confused.

I read it without a thought. Shikha was the first to laugh whole heartedly. Everyone else did too once they heard my answer. I pretended to laugh at myself as well. That was real embarrassing but I had to put up a fake smile, as if it was a part of the lighter moment I created in a serious Aptitude class. Honestly, I was sweating as well. I saw Shikha laughing and glowing. She was not only pretty, but intelligent as well. Out of forty students, only the two of us could solve the problem. I was proud of her.

We came out and she laughed as we walked to the nearest coffee shop.

She asked me, “How did you guess the correct answer?” I looked at her and said with a straight face, “The number 415 was my role number during college and I was the odd one sitting over there with you. Did you get it?” I said in a shrill tone, still reeling from the experience. She realized I was still anxious. Seeing me like that, she teased me again.

“Aww…my sweetie… You need some strawberry again…”

She punched me hard and held my hand. I loved it.

“By the way, do you know when couples hold each other’s hands so tightly? Can you guess?” she asked mischievously, clutching my hand tightly. I smiled as I whispered.

“Love making at its best.”

And our voices faded as we walked quietly. It was soothing even though it was a hot afternoon at Rajiv Chowk.

The Doubt and Love making

It was during one of our long conversations during the day time that I told her everything about Eva and Aridhita. She listened to me patiently. I honestly confessed everything I had been through. Once I was done, she asked me quite a few questions. She was a typical fiery character, most of the time unpredictable, but the real part was that she was too lovable to be ignored. I couldn't ignore her when she asked me many things out of the blue and I couldn't relate where they ended with the same topic that I had started with her.

"Do your office friends know about me?" she asked me.

"No, I never share my personal life with them," I calmly replied feeling proud about the space I have kept for my private life with respect to my professional life.

"Why haven't you told anyone?" she enquired.

"What should I tell them and about whom?" I asked getting confused.

"Who is Jaspreet?" she asked out of nowhere. I was perplexed. How did she get to know her name when I never told her.

"She sits with our team and on our floor. But why are you asking me about her and how do you know her name?"

"I found a letter written by you for her in your pen drive. You have written down all your feelings and love for her. What should I conclude from that?" she asked, her face clouded with doubt.

I remembered I had lent her my pen drive. I had saved the letter I had written for Gowtham on it. The unfortunate part was that in my hurry, I had signed my name at the end of the letter. It took me half an hour to convince her that it had nothing to do with me. Even then, I don't know whether I had managed to convince her.

"Are you interested only in a casual fling even now? Hook around, then leave and hurt someone?" she asked again.

"No, not at all. I never did even earlier, so how can I do it now? I think no matter how hard I try, I get trapped by emotions and hurt myself," I said explaining to her my intentions. I was worried as I didn't want her to think ill of me.

"Then why did you kiss Eva and Aridhita?" she asked and I went quiet. There was an awkward silence for a moment before I tried explaining to her.

"I never kissed them intentionally. That just happened. In fact, I never forced anyone or had any ill intentions against them. I was just helping them…" I couldn't complete my sentence when she cut me short.

"Helping them? By kissing them? By hugging them? By holding someone by the waist in a crowded place? You must be doing the same with the girls in your team, especially Jaspreet. Are you a kid who can be dragged and fooled around with?" she asked raising her voice. I was feeling terrible, because I couldn't figure out what she was heading towards. It was true I wasn't a kid. I guess she was also annoyed when I told her about Pallavi,

Chiya and the other girls in my team who were good friends of mine.

"No Shikha, what's wrong with you? There was nothing like that. And my teammates are very good friends and..." I began before I was interrupted.

"I know what you guys want. You are just passing time with me as well. If you care a bit for me, then have guts to admit to your team that you are with me," she said and disconnected the phone.

I don't know what I had achieved by confessing to her, but for the first time I noticed a different Shikha. The strong stubborn, straightforward, blunt and bold girl was sounded insecure and vulnerable. I tried calling her, but she didn't answer. I tried concentrating on my work, but couldn't. What was her agenda? Did she want me to say something to her? Was she seeking something from me? Why was she confusing me? Was it time to confess that I was falling for her, but that was the same case with her I guess. There were all these thoughts running in my mind when I received a message from her.

I am sorry for being rude. I will be at the entrance of your office in a moment. See you soon. I am missing you.

It was like an energy drink and it charged me. I was happy again. I quickly winded up all the work and it was exit time by then. The whole team got up with me, including Gowtham, Chiya, Pallavi, my lead, the manager and a few others. I quickly went to the canteen to buy some chocolates for her. I got her favourite blueberry ice-cream packed as well when I received her call that she was just outside.

She was dressed in a white top with black hot pants. Her hair was wet and untied. I could see the guards looking at her. I ran towards her waving with a big smile on my face when I saw my manager with Pallavi and Chiya. They were walking parallel to me and I abruptly hid my face. They didn't see me but Shikha noticed the change in my expression; she saw me hiding my face with the packets I had in my hand. The entrance was at an equal distance from me and my team. Shikha was just outside the entrance. I turned my face the other way only to hear Shikha shouting my name aloud. Not only did my manager notice me hiding, but people along the corridor stopped to stare. I was literally praying that my manager should leave. At that point I remembered the fight that I had had with Shikha about telling my teammates about her. Was that why she was outside my office? What should I do now? I could not ignore her as it was loud and clear that she was calling my name as well as pointing towards me. Before I could react and run away, I turned and found my manager standing next to me, with Gowtham and Chiya to his left and Pallavi laughing half-heartedly standing to his right.

"Hey man! Why are you in an awkward position?" Gowtham giggled and asked, embarrassing me.

"Nothing. I was on a call… I was thinking about something…." I tried explaining the situation. I could see Chiya and Pallavi trying to control their giggles. Meanwhile, my manager turned towards Shikha and signalled to the guards to let her in. She was over excited as though she had got an entry into an arena to meet some celebrity. I was mortified. She came running and half-hugged me, snatching the ice cream and box of chocolates from me. I tried to be normal when I introduced her to my teammates. It was like she already knew everybody through me. She greeted them well and they all seemed to get along with each other.

"Is she the reason that you are making a lot of mistakes in your code?" my manager whispered to me.

"No sir, not at all," I said confidently.

"That's fine, but she is worth it even if you are committing mistakes because of her," Mr. Teja stated, smiled and gave me a high five. Shikha seemed to have mingled well. In a flash, she was discussing the earrings Pallavi was wearing, praising the new dress which Chiya had worn that day and and teased Gowtham. We all moved out. Shikha was with me, holding my hand tightly

Everyone left and Shikha was feeling on top of the world. It was as though she had accomplished a mission. No doubt I loved it; the authority with which she was taking charge and driving was adorable. I was smiling and she was constantly blabbering about what her day had been like, telling me about her class, how few guys in the class tried on her and making me feel jealous by saying how lucky I was that she was with me ignoring hot guys in the class. We kept on walking and she kept on talking. Laxmi Nagar was a crowded place. We crossed the subzi mandi which was buzzing with vendors and buyers. She was saying something when she noticed a vendor displaying Indian plums and fresh red cherries. She suddenly exclaimed, "I love cherries!" and quickly grabbed a few from the cart and started running away, leaving me with the angry vendor.

"*Saheb, apni maidam ko bolo kuch akal karo, gareeb ka nuksaan kyu karte ho.*"

I couldn't react and paid him, when Shikha beckoned me.

"Why did you have to steal? He was furious," I said getting irritated.

"It's okay, chill! Sometimes stealing is fun. Here take some. They are so good."

She pacified me and kissed me on my cheek, that too when the street was crowded. We walked for a few minutes before we reached her flat. I was about to leave when she handed me her flat keys.

"You are not going anywhere. Take these keys, keep them with you. Come after ten minutes and don't follow me," she said quickly.

"But what will your roommates think? It is not right," I said though I wanted to come.

"They are gone till Monday. So my lover boy, we have loads of time to have fun," she stated teasing me and before I could say anything, she added, "Listen, I stay on the 3rd floor. Don't write down your name on the entry register. See you," she said and ran away leaving me standing there wondering whether it was a wise idea; the guard was watching both of us. I was sure that he knew what we were up to.

I reached her flat after half an hour, trying not to be noticed by the guard but in vain as he stopped me and asked, "*Wo nikar wali madam ke pass ja rahe sir ji?*" he asked in a Haryanvi accent. He was in his mid forties.

"Yes, do you mind?" I asked getting a little defensive.

"*Mind wind na kare se, hari patti dikha do sir ji,*" he asked for a bribe shamelessly. I smiled and gave him a hundred rupee note reluctantly. I didn't want any trouble. Shikha had told me that the building rules were strict, but I could see how easily they could be breached.

I reached her flat. It was rather messy. The drawing hall was small and there were bras and other garments put out to dry. She asked me to sit in her room. It had an attached washroom. It was a small flat but Shikha's room was well kept. She had put a few charts on the wall on which she had written down her daily schedule. There were the multiplication tables charts, mathematical formulae charts and a few analytical charts covering stats and figures. She had kept the basket and the teddy bear I had given to her right at the center of her table, along with the card. It had a note that said 'Gift from my Mr Amateur'. I saw a beautiful ring kept beside it. It looked like an expensive diamond ring.

I had a bath before dinner. After chatting for a while, Shikha got down to study as she had a test the next day. I was feeling tired and don't know when I dozed off.

"Hey... lover boy...hellooo..." she whispered sitting close to me. I opened my eyes rubbing them softly when she kissed my eyes and whispered, "How rude! How can you ignore someone like me. Look at you sleeping as if you don't even care?"

I realized it was close to midnight. I had slept for two hours. The lights had been dimmed. As I regained my senses fully, I looked at Shikha. Wow! She was wearing a purple coloured transparent baby doll night dress. They revealed her smooth waxed legs. The dress was made for mischievous canoodling under the sheets. The colour of her inner wear were the same, The dress donned so perfectly on her slim body that all I could do was hold her tightly and kiss her passionately.

I looked deep into her eyes as I held her softly from her waist and made her lie on the bed. I slid on top of her, careful enough to not to press my body against her. Slightly caressing her silky hair, I kissed her forehead, moving my fingers softly around her cheeks. She sighed and her eyes seemed to be asking for more. Starting from her forehead, with a touch skillful enough to produce a sensation in her body and her eyes talking, I placed my lips softly on her enigmatic eyes, her cheeks, and her chin. I lowered her body over mine gently. My fingers felt her neck, and rolled towards her shoulders sliding from her left arm to hold her hand tightly when she whispered.

"When do we hold our hands tightly like this?"

"You are looking beautiful," I whispered without answering her and she blushed.

"While making love," I whispered into her left ear and kissed it. I proceeded to kiss her neck and then her shoulders. She released my hand and it moved towards her waist pressing it down towards her half folded left leg. I felt her thighs as my hand slid under her dress. I moved my hand up her back and unhooked her bra. We were drowned in each other, the heat was high, the moment was light, the sound was rhythmic, the breeze was fragrant, and all inhibitions were removed. I sensed her quivering lips and could smell the strawberry flavored lip balm. I removed her bra and held her tight. She lifted herself slightly to reach my lips. They touched mine and opened. I could feel her heart beating hard against my chest. She was breathing fast as the moment came when we kissed passionately, losing ourselves in the heat of the moment.

When Gowtham Left

Gowtham was still waiting for a reply from Jaspreet. He had mailed her the letter after editing it. Finally Jaspreet had replied. Gowtham couldn't sleep that night as he was over excited; he kept discussing how he would talk to her, where he would take her for their first date, where he'd propose to her as she had asked him to meet her after office.

I was very happy for him as I listened to him making his plans as excited as a child. I thought of proposing to Shikha as well. It was going to be August in a few days. Her birthday month and I decided to propose to her on her birthday to make the day even more special. I was almost drowned in her thoughts every moment of the day. I wanted to talk to her that night as well but Shikha seemed preoccupied. She told me she had come from the market when I called her twice, but she rejected my calls. She messaged me that she was feeling too tired to talk to me at that moment so I left a text for her. I realized that I had gotten so used to talking to her every night and sharing all my thoughts over the last few months that going to bed without talking to her seemed like a major disruption in my routine. I was missing her terribly. I understand that we all need our own space at times. Gowtham slept peacefully but I couldn't.

It was the first time that Gowtham had not sleep talked or snored. The sense of achieving his girl was quite satisfying; he must have been dreaming about her. I on the other hand was so excited about her birthday, I couldn't sleep. I decided to sketch something for her instead.

It was Thursday and I was waiting for Gowtham. He had gone out for the first time with Jaspreet, so even I was excited. They didn't go far as Gowtham had taken her to the nearby Coffee House after office. He wanted to go somewhere close by so that he could spend more time with her rather than getting to the place. Jaspreet, a typical Punjabi beauty, was wearing a peach coloured kurti, jeans and her long hair was tied. I chatted with her for a bit before I excused myself.

Gowtham whispered to me, "Oh man! Don't even think about her else I will tell Shikha."

He made me laugh. I said goodbye to them and left to meet Shikha. She was unusually quiet that day. The spark on her face was missing. She was upset about something and that was clear on her face. I tried talking about my day, asked her about her class and then about her birthday to make her feel good, but nothing worked. We were sitting near the area between V3S Mall and Scope Minar. I couldn't resist asking her what the matter was.

"Is everything fine?"

"No, nothing is going well," she said abruptly. It was evident that she was not one of those people who pretend to be fine when they are not. Her expressions were sad, her face was burdened with something, she didn't even tie her hair that day, they were rough, and her eyes were swollen as if she had been crying the whole night. There was definitely something troubling her.

"I am not going in the right direction. I came away from my hometown to do something meaningful, but there seems to have been no progress," she lamented. I waited for her to continue so that I could figure out what her problem was.

"I feel like I am hardly concentrating on my studies and I am wasting my time. I failed in the tests yesterday, and the ones day before yesterday..." she paused and then continued.

"I am unable to move on and I don't know what I am doing here," she stated, clearly sounding frustrated. I was left wondering if I was the reason of her sudden lack of concentration in her studies. I was feeling stifled inside. Would she stop meeting me? Would she say that she needed to concentrate on her studies? There was every possibility of taking a decision in haste with her.

Why can't every love story run smoothly? Just when you think everything is going hunky dory, something turns up to hit you hard. Either of the two will be hurt by any means, by deliberate acts or non-wishfully to take each other to the void where one should say 'I am done with life'. I couldn't think about anything but said what I felt should be said at that time, ready to face the outcome...whatever it may be.

"If you feel that I am responsible for wasting your time, then I feel we shouldn't meet. You should study hard and achieve what you came for," I said quietly. I didn't want her to do it, but I had to offer a selfless solution. She looked at me with razor sharp eyes and she lashed out at me.

"Did I ask you for advice? Are you a '*daanveer*' who wants to make a sacrifice? The fact that I shared my problem with you doesn't mean that I want you to go away..." she paused and looked at me with piercing eyes. I must admit I was feeling better. I was still quiet when she continued, "Do you truly want me to go away? Are you fine if we stop meeting each other?"

she asked seeking an honest reply. I shook my head briefly and looking into her eyes.

"Then shut up! Let's go for a walk."

I didn't say a word. We walked together till the metro station. It was a quiet walk. She held my hand and I felt good. She was feeling better, I could see. Though I couldn't provide any solution to the problem, the fact that she had vented her frustration made her relax. At the same time, I felt that there was something else and this wasn't the only thing that was hurting her. I knew her then and the real Shikha was lost I guess. Things had changed after the night we spent together at her flat. The fun loving, sharp, bubbly, restless and excited Shikha was lost, thinking, mourning over something inside. She wasn't the sort of character who would cry or explain everything in detail. She was a strong girl who would fight on her own till the end. I, however, was feeling insecure.

I reached home after dropping her. I was supposed to wait for Gowtham, but he had decided to spend some more time with Jaspreet. Shikha was still lost in her own thoughts. Though she had said the reason was her worry about her studies, I wasn't convinced. It's just that when you get involved with someone you tend to develop an intuitive power about them. You tend to read them better than they read themselves and I knew there was another reason for her change in behaviour.

Gowtham reached home and I tried putting aside my thoughts of Shikha. I was really happy for him and the moment he entered, he held out his fingers.

"Choose one out of the two fingers," he stated calmly, giving me two options in the form of his index finger and middle finger to choose from. Without further questioning and probing, I quietly chose the index finger.

"Oh, that's sad news. If you would have chosen the middle finger, it would have been good news for you… for me, I mean," he jumped in excitement pointing his middle finger at me. I was happy to see him excited.

"Now can you please break the suspense?" I asked raising my eye brows in rage.

"Seri… seri. Let me give you the good news, though not related to you. Jaspreet liked ıny company today and she said that she will miss me. She has become my very good friend and aii am so happy," he said and I just gestured asking him to share the sad news when I got up from my bed to get the glass of water.

"The sad news is that I will be leaving Delhi forever as I have been released from my project. I am moving to Chennai," he said quietly. I was stunned. I felt as if something had broken or shattered. I had a glass of water in my hand. I paused myself for a few seconds, turned back pretending to be normal and smiled at him.

"When did you ask for a release from the project and why didn't you tell me?" I questioned without showing any emotion.

"I applied a few weeks ago and didn't get a chance to tell you. Oh man, you were always lost in Shikha. You'd come home late. I didn't get time to speak to you, but that's okay," he stated plainly. It was true. I had really been involved with Shikha and had hardly spent any time with him in the past few months. Even when I was home, I'd always be on the phone with her. I couldn't manage time on weekends when Gowtham was left with no other option but to visit relatives every time as I remained occupied with Shikha. I felt a little guilty but tried to be normal.

"So when are you leaving Delhi?" I asked arranging the bed sheet.

"I am leaving on Saturday," he said and I nodded with a smile. He was leaving in two days! That came as an absolute shock. I didn't react. I could only gesture to him to switch off the lights, showing that I was feeling sleepy. He switched off the lights and went to his own room. I stayed awake. I was suddenly feeling burdened. Gowtham would be leaving on Saturday and Shikha had not called. I did, but she didn't pick up her phone. She just messaged to say that she was studying. Emotions were running amok in my head. I tossed and turned the entire night.

The last two days with Gowtham flew by. We were together most of the time. I would help him pack at night. We, however, hardly talked as Gowtham seemed lost. There was a lot to talk and discuss, but nothing was striking at that moment when we were thinking about the last nostalgic moments. Finally the day of his departure arrived. Shikha came along with me to drop him at the New Delhi railway station. The whistle of the engine was loud and clear. The signal was green and I waved a final goodbye to Gowtham. I could see the tears in his eyes though he was hiding them. He had always wanted to go back to *'maai Tamil, maai Tirupur, maai lovely district'*. His heart was clearly aching though. I wanted to say many things to him – a special thanks and a special goodbye, but I pretended to be my normal self trying to joke around, tease him and pull his leg. He wasn't shouting or laughing but was replying with a quiet smile. He was finally gone, the train disappeared and I was left with Shikha.

"Are you fine?" she asked and I nodded with a smile. We walked quietly till the metro station. We boarded the metro and then I dropped her till the exit gate at the metro station.

"I wish you could come with me right now. It's your birthday tomorrow," I said expressing my desire.

"I want to, but I have to attend my class. I will come in the evening for sure. And I know it's my birthday. See you at nine," she smiled and pulled my nose.

I felt a little better but she didn't seem to be excited at all. She was quiet when we met in the morning. Even when we went to drop Gowtham, she didn't say much. I guess she was still worried and I hoped to change her mood by celebrating her birthday. I left waving at her and she hugged me. She went off but didn't look back. That was something she usually did.

I reached home but I missed Gowtham. I was missing Shikha as well. I couldn't believe that he was gone. I had planned on celebrating her birthday with Gowtham, but he wasn't there. It felt as though he would walk in at any moment. I was feeling as if it was a nightmare. I sat for a moment. It was 4 o' clock by then and I was somewhere in a state of shock. I went in his room, switched on the light, and tried feeling his presence. I was thinking he might pop up from behind or he might come out of the washroom, giving me a surprise, but that wasn't the case. We had not been able to even talk properly in the past few days. I was so into Shikha that I had ignored Gowtham. Now he was gone. We had surely had some fun times together. I was sure he was missing me as well. I decided to celebrate Shikha's birthday in Gowtham's room so that he could be with us in spirit.

I had already made the arrangements for her birthday. I blew up a few heart shaped balloons and fixed them around the room. A few I left on the floor. I had made a sketch for her which I had framed. It was wrapped and ready. She said she loved roses so I got a bouquet for her. It was the moment that I was waiting for. It was her reaction. I hoped that it would help us through the rough patch. As I readied the room, the more hopeful, confident and excited I became. It was eight o'clock when I called her to ask her where she was.

"Hey, I am just done with the class. I scored well today," she said. She didn't sound very excited but at least she was talking. I was happy.

"Great! Hope you are fine. When can I expect you here?" I asked getting energetic.

"Well… I am going home first to get ready. Give me two hours. I will call you once I reach," she said calmly.

I was joyful. I checked the clock again. The next two hours were going to be the toughest, waiting for her. I thought of practicing the same song that I had left incomplete the last time. So I took my guitar and began to sing. The weather had changed outside. The sky was filled with dark clouds. It was going to rain and I was happy and felt the sudden change of weather might bring a positive change in my life. I started getting ready. I got myself a new pair of jeans and a new shirt. I decided to hide the gifts in different places in the room. I chose the drawer near Gowtham's study table. I opened the drawer to place the sketch in it when I found a blue diary with something written on it in Tamil. Gowtham must have forgotten it. I was about to ping him when I casually opened it. I had opened a page with the bookmark. I was in for a surprise. It was a message for me.

Dear Best Friend,

I never thought of loving the north side, neither was I fascinated by this location till I met you. If I would ever love to thank anyone, that would be the MNC which sent me here so that I could meet you, You got super busy with that haat chick…oohh I love it. I know you were always seeking someone and I am happy you got one; she seems to be the best girl for you. Don't lose her like you lost the others, else I'll kill you. Thanks for Jaspreet's letter. Alaga irrukada avaa. Oh man, I am sorry. It means 'she is beautiful'.

I know I will not be able to say anything to you when we will part so I chose to write, and I am sure you will read it soon. Remember the thought you induced in me: when love meets ego? I learnt a lot from it, and I never feared losing her or getting hurt because I love her. So no Ego, only Love for my cute Punjabi girl. And hope to see you soon my friend. Thanks for tolerating my talking in my sleep and snoring.

I love Tamil, my Tirupur, my lovely district and I love Delhi now and I love you as well.

Miss you friend,

Gowtham

His letter touched me. I closed my eyes and whispered the same. I kept his diary safely with me. He was a special friend. I remembered all the times we had shared. I was feeling low and hoped that Shikha would turn up soon. Celebrating her birthday would make me feel better. It was close to eleven when I ordered dinner and a few snacks. I lay the dinner table with new mats, a flower vase, a candle stand and a birthday card. I was ready! I looked at the clock and called her. The phone rang five times before she disconnected it. She must be nearby I thought and relaxed. However, half an hour went by and there was no sign of her. I felt something was wrong. I called her again but her phone was switched off.

I rose from my chair. I was rather worried now. I hoped nothing had happened to her. I started cursing myself for letting her come alone at this time. It was raining heavily as well. The battery of her phone must have run out or maybe she had misplaced her phone. There were hundreds of 'maybes' running in my head. There were just five minutes left for the clock to strike twelve. I hoped that she was planning a last minute entry, but nothing of that sort happened. I was getting edgy. I was sweating in fear and I called her more than fifty times…all in vain. I even emailed her and left a chat message but did not get a reply. Each passing second was taking its toll on me. I didn't know what to do next. I sat in the corner of the room and stared at candles and flowers on the table. It was three in the morning. I felt I was alone in a place haunted by demons, a place where fear is the biggest monster which can kill you.

It was half past three when my phone rang. I jumped up with a start. I ran to pick it up from the study table. 'Shikha calling' flashed on the screen. I was relieved. I picked it up and gushed, "Happy birthday to you, Shikha. Hope you are fine and where were you?"

I didn't get any response. I took her name a few times when a male voice shouted at me.

"What have you done? Shikha has committed suicide because of you. I will not leave you!"

I became numb. I couldn't believe what he had just said to me. I couldn't breathe. I couldn't say a word. I regained my senses when he shouted 'hello' many times and I finally asked him.

"Who are you?"

"I am Ritesh. Shikha's fiancé."

The Suicide Note and the final Good Bye

It was 4.15 a.m. and still dark outside. It was raining heavily. I had the keys of her flat with me. I knew there was something wrong. She wasn't weak to have committed such a horrendous act. The guard with his usual uniform sagging from his shoulders, and half a beedi sandwiched between his lips, gave me a rusty look through his half-open eyes. I took the lift till her third floor apartment and was completely drenched. I was shedding water all over the lift floor. The sound of the falling raindrops was crystal clear and it seemed to be a never-ending rainfall with lightening striking before the thundering burst of clouds. It was a shocker for me. I could hardly imagine her not being with me now… when I had seen her yesterday itself. The lift halted and I stepped out in a hurry, almost running in the direction of her flat with one hand in my pocket, pulling out the keys. The door made a creaky sound after I unlocked it. I switched on the lights and made my way towards her bedroom. My eyes were eagerly searching for something; there must have been a certain reason for her sudden act. I searched the drawer, under the table, her almirah, her bags with the hope of discovering anything that could at least tell me something that might have happened in the last twenty-four hours. But I had to give up my search and couldn't do much. I dropped myself on the couch with tired hands covering my face but eyes still trying to locate something that could pacify me. Every register on the table and piecc of paper near the dustbin under the study table kept near her bed made me think that it might be containing the note written by her, but then the immediate thought of it having been explored already ended my hopes. It made me more restless and panic-stricken; someone could be knocking at the door anytime. Leaving all hopes of getting anything, I was about to leave when I found a blue LED blinking under the bed. I guess it was her laptop. I immediately ran to pick it up as it was connected with the charger. It was in sleep mode so I had to restart it. I saw a few tabs open in the task bar. One of them was a folder with her name, then Internet Explorer Gmail icon, and the last was the Outlook mail icon. I clicked the last one and came across her inbox which had last mail received from Ritesh. I checked her sent items and found nothing that could give me a lead. Finally my eyes did find something in the Outbox folder and there it was showing the five mails which were still in queue to be sent to the desired address. They must have been left unsent due to a broken connection somewhere at that point of time. It was showing under the sent column and my eyes slowly moved towards the 'To' column to check the addressed name. It was my ID. I was shocked to check the first unsent mail with the subject: **'I am done- Goodbye forever'**. I double clicked to check the contents. Fearing someone would come, I copied the mail and saved it in the pen drive attached. Just then, the power went off with loud thunder and before I could read anything, the laptop got switched off. Damn, it was only working well with the charger on. I kept everything aside, ejected the pen drive and ran out in a flash.

I had a hard time making my way back home from her flat. As soon as I reached my place, I took my laptop to check the pen drive. My hands were quivering. I opened the drive, double clicked on the icon which I had saved and could see the subject line 'I am done - Goodbye forever'.

Dear Amateur,

I loved calling you by this name as I have always told you. I know you must hate me for what you will be going through because of me. I wanted to share many things with you, but I feared to do so. I never wanted to lose you on bad terms. The time we spent together was all I had. You had completely taken over my heart and I was so into you that I couldn't resist falling for you. I loved teasing you, correcting you, sharing things with you, holding your hand tightly, and going around with you. I loved our conversations, your special attention towards me and our kisses. It was going fine till my past started haunting me again.

He came back out of nowhere and I went into a state of confusion. He is Ritesh, the guy who ruled my life for the past three years. He was my first love. There was something special about him when he proposed to me. Our journey together went on smoothly for a few years and then we got engaged. He used to take care of everything. He used to make me feel like a wonder girl, but as they say, nothing is perfect till it is tested at the right time. He failed the test of time. He became wayward, he neglected me, he didn't keep his promises, he got distracted and cheated on me. I had trusted him so I couldn't take it and I went into acute depression. The days started to haunt me, the nights were sleepless and time stood still. My body no longer seemed mine. I felt as if I had been used and discarded. I couldn't shake off that feeling. I slapped him and insulted him when he came back and apologized. But the pain had penetrated into my heart. I never wanted to see his face and he was gone. I couldn't move on though and lay wasted at home. I knew I was being unfair to my parents. I was hurting them by being selfish. It was then when I wasted a year doing nothing that my parents decided to send me to Mumbai to my relative's home for a change. I joined a rehabilitation center to get back on track. I learnt a lot and I slowly came out of it. It was then that I met you in the train from Bandra to Delhi where we had a chat and I told you to never to fall in love as love never wins over ego, and it hurts. I never imagined that I would come in contact with you through that blog. It was when I found your blog titled 'When Love Meets Ego' I got tempted to comment on it. I thought there must be a connection. When I saw your profile picture I recognized you and made contact.

After we began corresponding, I started getting addicted to you. It was special and I loved you. But then Ritesh came back. He contacted my family and so did his family. He was always in my mind as I couldn't completely forget him. He met me last week and he cried like a child. He confessed, he regretted his behavior and he promised to be there for me forever. But then it was you who was ruling my heart and mind. The moments spent with you were special and fresh. It was confusion between my past and present; I wanted to live in the present but never wanted to lose my past. I was struggling, I was confused and I hated myself for dragging you in the midst of it. I explained everything to Rithesh. I told his parents about you as well. They were ready to accept me even after hearing the truth. Everything would be fine if I could forget you. I had got him back, our families were reunited and I would be marrying him. But your memories were confusing me. I couldn't explain it all to you and I don't think I would have been able to face you. The guilt was taking its toll on me. It was excruciating and was questioning my integrity.

I was not fake with you; I valued you and loved you. What we had was real. So keeping in mind the respect and love I shared with you, I would like to say sorry to you. If possible please forgive me. By the time you will read this letter, I will be gone from your life but I will be watching you. Don't curse me; the only way I can get a smile to you is by giving up my life.

Miss You Lover Boy,

Your Contemporary Brat,

Shikha

I could not believe that she had been going through so much. I didn't even have an inkling of anything. Why did she have to choose to take the foolish and easier way of escaping things? I wanted to be with her. I never wanted to lose her. I could still feel her hugs and those kisses. How could she leave me? I wish she could have told me and I would have asked her to go back to him without any hard feelings. Or I might have asked her to stay with me and leave him. We could have at least talked about it. Why did she have to kill herself? I was feeling giddy. I hadn't slept and my body was aching, but I wanted to see her. I chose to leave my flat and headed towards her place again.

The Last Meeting

It was early morning. I was not nervous at all. I wanted to see her face. I wanted to see her. It would be tough but I had to see her for the last time. Though I might not get the answers, I wanted to at least face something bitter with courage. I bribed and got the details from the watchman of her building. I reached the hospital where she had been taken. He told me that she had consumed rat poison. Her fiancée and his family were present at that time and they brought her to the hospital. No case was registered. They had handled it pretty well. They brought her well in time and rest was all taken care of by a few well managed statements and money. The lady at the reception gave me details about the room and I ran towards it.

I almost reached the room when I saw her from afar. It was a great relief to see her breathing. She was looking her cute self. She was lying on the bed and a guy was sitting on her left. A lady in her mid-forties was feeding her something from a bowl. She was active enough to wipe her lips with her hands after having her liquid diet. They seemed happy to get their daughter back. I was feeling left out and the odd man facing the united team. I didn't go any closer as it would be embarrassing to face them all. They might or might not know me. I was holding a small bouquet with light flowers in it. Before I could ask someone to deliver it to her from my side, I heard my name and everybody started staring at me. Shikha gestured to the guy sitting next to her and within a minute, everybody moved out. As they walked out of the room, I could see shikha as the pampered child that everybody followed without questioning. Or perhaps they didn't want to question at that critical point of time. Everyone moved out and looked at me; one of the old couples gave me a warm welcoming smile. I greeted all of them with a *namaste.* The guy came out last. He held her hand tightly and kissed her forehead. As he walked past me, he stared hard. I kept calm and took my eyes off him. I went towards Shikha and sat beside her. I was trying to be courageous, but my heart was beating fast. A day earlier, she had been my girl and now I was a mere stranger standing like a fool. She smiled and said hello. It was a formal one. She was looking at me with deep innocent eyes and I tried to not to make eye contact.

"So how was your test and class?" I blurted like an idiot. I felt awkward as though I was speaking to a stranger.

"What will I do with an MBA test, when I have failed the test of my life?" she answered and I couldn't resist a slight smile thinking about the philosophy she was trying to imply at the situation.

"Don't worry. It happens," I said and I kept my hand on her forehead. When I looked at her, my eyes penetrated into hers and I was lost again. She was feeling sad while I was angry. I wanted to ask her so many questions.

Why? Why did you have to do this? Why did you contact me? Why did you have to use me and ease your pain to satisfy your ego?

But I couldn't say anything. I kept a smile on my face, caressing her head when she started to feel weaker and her eyes welled up with tears.

"I love you and I wasn't using you. Please forgive me," she uttered as if she had read my mind. My smile faded and there was a definite turn in my expression to something surprising.

No, I can't forgive you. Why should I? Why were you angry at Eva and Aridhita when they were with me? You are no different. You did the same. At least they admitted what they had done.

"You must be thinking that I am like Eva and that other girl whom you helped, Aridhita," she said as I looked at her in surprise. She remembered their names as well. I was still looking at her as my hand caressed her cheeks. She turned her face and kissed my hand.

"No no... I don't even remember them," I said trying to bring a smile on her face. But my mind was saying something different.

Okay, please don't be that sweet, or else I will forgive you. I wish you had come yesterday. I had arranged everything. I had made a sketch for you. I had practiced that song for you. I wanted to wish and celebrate your birthday and I wanted to hug you, kiss you and propose to you. I could have given you the best time, but why did you even think of quitting in between? You spoilt everything, Shikha, why didn't you tell me?

"I wanted to come to you. I never knew he would come. I wanted him back and he was in my mind all the time. I failed you. I am poor girl."

As she said this, she started crying. I had to forget everything to console her and give her selfless advice. I still remember when I had given her the same when we had met for the first time in the train.

You are thinking too much. You should relax and if he is a nice guy, you should give him a chance. You never know what and where your story can go!

I gave her the same advice. This time also, it was genuine selfless advice that tore away my heart and mind. I was sure this time she won't do anything completely opposite to what I suggest. I realized it was time to leave and go away from her life forever. I took out her gift which I had made for her. It was the sketch.

"Hey Shikha, a last gift to you from your Lover Boy!" I managed to grab her attention. She looked into my eyes and I could feel her beauty, the mesmerizing eyes which were so genuine, honest, deep and far too beautiful to be resisted. She asked me to open the gift for her. It was the sketch of a guy staring at a girl lost in prayer with folded hands. Shikha saw and she smiled. I guess she recalled the moment when we had met at the Iskcon temple. I wished her good luck and gestured to her to leave when she asked me.

"Will you miss me?"

I didn't say anything but I noticed tears trickling down her cheeks. I was trying hard to be strong, selfless and normal. Oh God! Everything seemed to be haunting me at that time. In a flash I saw the time spent with her – her arrival at the Iskcon temple when she met me for the first time, when she was praying, when she laughed when she played the prank on me, when she kissed me for the first time, when she forced me to attend a class with her, her lip gloss, her smile, her laugh, her fights, her questions, and my answers. Now I would be out from her life. That situation was really testing me and I couldn't bear it anymore. It was getting tougher for me to hold back my tears. I kissed her forehead and whispered.

"I will try to miss you."

I quickly got up and without looking at her left the room. I didn't bother to look at anyone standing in my way either. I headed towards my flat and on the way home, I decided to visit the Iskcon temple.

The journey was long and I reassessed what I had gone through. It all started with the casual fling I wanted to be in, but ended up falling in love again. I met a few bruised egos and I was sure that there must be many people going through the same ordeal. If I will be hurt by someone, I will hurt someone else directly or indirectly. Love exists in bits and pieces and the rest is just pleasure with pain. Had there been love, there would have been the 'let them go' feeling, but how many of us actually believe in this thought today? You let go of your love and you will only end up getting hurt. People want to have someone static with them, their one true love and other as a fling who can satisfy their ego. The rope of attachment is nothing but a hurt ego that never gets pacified till both experiment, fall for attraction and attain the same.

I was left with no energy to even talk to anyone. I was hurt but I was in no mood to hurt anyone or find leisure or even love. I entered the temple and it was the same time of the evening aarti that Shikha and I had attended. I was missing her and I knew I won't be able to see her again. Even if she would try to contact me, I decided not to respond. I didn't feel like going home; I was missing Gowtham as well. The time spent with both of them was unforgettable and it was lacerating me. I was thinking about my last conversation with her when I wanted to say something else to her. I wanted to tell her at least once how much I loved her and how much I cared. The feelings were left buried inside; my heart was aching and my throat chocked when I folded my hands and stood in front of the supreme lord asking for peace. I couldn't control myself when I cried.

God : *Hey son!*

Me : *I am not in a good mode. I feel deprived and shattered.*

God : *That is the basic nature of every human being. No matter what we create for them, they still cry.*

Me : *We lose, that's why we cry.*

God : *Who said you owned anything in the first place.*

Me : *But…*

God : *It's written in the Gita, the Vedas, and any other holy books. But still people cry.*

Me : *Why do things have to happen when they have no end?*

God : *Do you think the end you wanted would have been the only end?*

Me : *If we can't decide the end, then why do we begin? What's the point of life then?*

God : *What's the fun of knowing the end? A game is half lost if you already know what the result will be.*

Me : *But we never get what we want…*

God : *Who said so? Didn't you get the casual fling you wanted since the beginning of your journey?*

Me : *But I thought that it would never hurt.*

God : *Who said what you desire will always have smooth roads? You always experience what you desire but that doesn't mean it will keep sticking to you. That's why one must have a clear intent and wise thoughts to choose from. Every thought you have has its consequences. Pain and pleasure are two sides of a coin. The way you had pleasure when you got what you wanted, you have to bear the pain related to that as well.*

Me : *What should I do? All this is hurting me.*

God : *Heal and hurt are parcels of life. Both teach you, make you stronger and better. Crying and complaining makes you weaker. Life will keep moving, but nothing will change till you keep on lamenting. Being stagnant will make you stink, so move ahead. Life will keep giving you reasons to live and survive and who knows when and where you will meet your happiness soon.*

Me : *But what if I would lose that again?*

God : *(smiling) I said you never lose anything because you never owned anything. You just experience, and experience remains. Stay blessed.*

My eyes were definitely swollen. I always used to wonder how people can cry while staring at an idol, but I got my answers. I opened my eyes only to be distracted by the sound of someone snapping their fingers.

"Hey! What are you doing here?" a woman's voice asked politely.

"Are you crying?" she asked. I turned around and looked at the woman. I was still confused and tried to recall where I had seen her. She was really familiar.

"Hi, I am Himansi. Hope you recognized me?" she asked. She was the same girl I had helped. I had given her a hundred rupees to save her from the auto driver. I smiled and nodded.

"I wanted to return your money as well. I came twice to your flat, but always found it locked," she said and we started moving out of the temple. She kept on talking and asked me umpteen questions, but I remained quiet.

"Where is your Tamil friend?"

"Where do you work?"

"Let me first tell you that I work at an MNC and you know we just shifted there last year."

"I love coming to Iskcon."

"'By the way, I forgot your name," she asked and finally I got a chance to say something.

"I am Krishna," I said and she smiled.

Enough of lamenting and crying over spilt milk. I turned back and looked at Krishna's idol. Even he was smiling. I could recall his message: *Life will keep giving you enough reasons to live and survive and who knows when and where you will meet your happiness soon.*

"By the way, even I love this place. I am also working in an MNC at Laxmi Nagar," I said smiling at her. We moved out of the temple premises to a stall of her favourite street food – pani-puri.

"Oh wow! But I work in Gurgaon," she said with a relentless smile. It was appealing and it was stable.

"Why were you crying?" she asked delicately.

"Aaah… I wasn't crying… I was praying and was a bit overwhelmed," I said calmly.

She was really pretty and sweet. Enough thoughts of hurt egos, casual flings and so on. Who knows where this story might go and who knows when and where Krishna may end up falling in love again….